Sea Spray and Woodland Glades

Edited by Mary Farrell

North Coast Writers

Graphic content and motifs designed by Sinead Coxhill, Mae Gardiner, Paul Girvan, Helen Hand, Yvonne Hamilton and Janet Peace.

ISBN: 978-1-915819-77-2

OTHER TITLES BY IMPSPIRED

Leviathan –
by Jae Jenkins-Scott

Specimens Under Glass -
by Mark Pearce

The Pinnacles of Hope –
by Charlie Brice

Maybury –
by Mary Farrell

SEE –
by John L. Stanizzi

Stepping Up –
by DC Diamondopolous

For Love of You –
by Ann Christine Tabaka

IMPSPIRED

All profits from this Anthology

will go to

two Charities

* * * * *

The British Heart Foundation

The RNLI

Contents

Pen & Paper

Robin Holmes

Geraldine Fleming

Sinead Coxhill

Mae Gardiner

Paul Girvan

Yvonne Hamilton

Brenda McAteer

Orla McFaul

Jimmy Milliken

Janet Peace

Sue Steging

Rhona Stephens

Sanderlings

Denise Ellis

Pam Leetch

Brendan Magee

Hazel Siberry

Words Inc

Maura Doran

Ruth Holloway

Kenny Campbell

Ian Garner

Editor - Mary Farrell

Acknowledgements of First Publication

Pen & Paper Acknowledgements:

Robin Holmes
Girona was published in *Resonance,* CAP Anthology, 2018.
Swallows, an Addendum was published in *Threshold,* CAP Anthology, 2022.
Primroses was published in *Compass*, CAP Anthology, 2023.

Geraldine Fleming
A Good Fermanagh Man and *A Slice of Soda* were first published in *Curiosity,* a collection of short stories by Geraldine Fleming, Impspired Press, 2023.
a rediscovered land was published in *Compass,* CAP Anthology, April 2023.
Arc of the Sun was published in *Fractured Echoes,* a collection of poetry by Geraldine Fleming, Impspired Press, 2023.
night driving was published in Paperclip Anthology, Ulster University, Summer 2023.

Sinead Coxhill
I Come From, December Sunset /January Sunset, Seascapes, Deserted were all published in *Menopausal Mermaids & Life lines*, a collection of work by Sinead Coxhill, Impspired Press, 2023.

Paul Girvan
Sour Grapes, Skellig Michael , Trouble up't Mill, The tentative subjunctive and *A-mused B-mused* were published in *A Time and Place,* Impspired Press, 2024

Orla McFaul
Balm was published in the Anthology *Love, Loss and Cardiac Issues*, Impspired Press, 2022.

Sue Steging
Four Stories About (The Same) Crows, recipient of the Seamus Heaney Award for New Writing, was published in *Compass*, CAP Anthology, 2023, as well as her poem *airborne*
Swallows was published in *The Bangor Literary Journal, Issue 18,* September 2022.
Secret Boxes was published in *Midsommar Night's Dream,* The Minison Project Magazine, Issue 3, October 2022.

Sanderlings Acknowledgements:

Brendan Magee
The Ring was published in *Flash Fiction Online Magazine,* 2019

Words Inc Acknowledgements:

Maura Doran
Golden Journey was first performed by Gemma Walker-Farren, in the Waterside Theatre Derry, Northern Ireland as the *Ninth Day of Christmas* in a *Twelve Days of Christmas* online performance, December 2020. It was later performed, by Maura, at a *Tenx9* event in Flowerfield Arts Centre Portstewart, Northern Ireland, May 2023.

* * * * *

Mary Farrell
A First of January Tale, Her New Whiskey Bottle, A Canine Acrostic, The Hawthorn Tree and *A Camino at St Anne's Cathedral* were published in *A Phoenix Still Rising,* a Collection by Mary Farrell, published by Impspired Press,2023

Introduction

By Mary Farrell

Welcome Readers to this third and last of the Anthologies garnered from Writers along the North Coast of Northern Ireland. There is much here which is familiar … and other features which are different. From these Anthologies you have come to expect a high standard of penmanship and a wide breath of content. The main difference is that there is now an augmented pool of contributing talent. Members of three different writing Groups are involved. We have entries from Pen and Paper (the u3a core Group of Writers featured in the first two Anthologies) as well as submissions from Sanderlings and Words Inc. Sanderlings is an independent writing Group which meets weekly in Portstewart, Northern Ireland. Words Inc is a Group run by Libraries NI in Coleraine, a few miles from Portstewart. Such a wealth of creativity is delivered to you here!

A wide array of topics is covered. Once more the familiar - surf and turf, birds and bees, family and friends, the sharing of life experiences and places visited. However, in this Anthology there are also numerous responses to Stimuli given in writing classes. We find prose and poems inspired by the works of well-known writers as well as pieces which have evolved from reactions to visual images. We follow intricate dialogues and the outlines of dramatically formatted shapes. All of these demonstrate the continuing courage of these Writers from the North Coast of Ireland to challenge themselves and try new styles and techniques.

So please laugh or sigh, remember or smile as you read, but above all, let these many voices touch you with their originality and authenticity.

~ from us to you ~

Robin Holmes

To everything there is a season

Robin Holmes believes that growing up on a small hill farm in the Mourne Mountains has been a deeply formative experience for his writing. In his poetry he explores themes of the natural world, the life of birds, the changing seasons and man's problematic relationship to the environment. His work has appeared regularly in the Bangor Literary Journal and in the annual Community Arts Partnership Anthologies, both Journals published in Northern Ireland. Video recordings of his poems '*Psithurism*' and '*Fred Dibnah*' are available on the Bangor Literary Journal's YouTube channel. His debut anthology '*The Shedding Gate*' was published by Impspired Press in April 2024.

FRED DIBNAH

Bolton born and bred
reared in a foundry
inherited the spirit of
Stephenson and Brunel
steeplejack jack of all trades
boiler suited flat capped
Lennon spectacled
self-taught but
oozed knowledge
charisma polished
with an oily rag
loved the pub
and a pint or two
travelled extensively
on his steam engine
Aveling and Porter, 1912
hands always black
with oil or coal
his world of grime
dovetailed onto television
crumpled political correctness
into his back pocket
unchanged by stardom
but cancer arrived
'Bloody hell '
blew a rivet in his boiler
thought nowt of it at first
but were only thing
he could not fix
or understand

GIRONA

On that night, the creaking, cracking and crumpling
of timbers; hull, bow and stern.
Masts scythed by the wind, falling as trees,
your sinking as assured as gravity.
Sailors diving into their salted graves
dug by a calamitous sea.
Lying for generations in the oceans tomb,
your timbers rotted, pulped and marinaded
in the bitter brine; the elements pestle and mortar
grinding away your destiny.

Until the Belgians came in 1968; a flotilla,
not an armada, armed with wet suits,
flippers, aqualungs, searchlights and cameras.
Fingers filtering through the slime, into
seaweed purses, gravel pouches, rocky chasms.
The ocean yielded up her secret hoard of
necklaces, brooches, amulets, torques,
salamanders of gold and
an engagement ring, enigmatic, engraved,
which when cleaned and polished, began to sing
a song unheard for centuries,
"I have nothing more to give Thee."
A melody composed, notated and scored
by the black, mournful, basalt sea.

THE BROAD STONE

Broad Stone, on the Long Mountain,
You are a Court Cairn, resembling a Portal Dolmen.
Before the Pyramids you were, and
after the Moon Landings you remain.
Your capstone is a timeless table, a
stone diaphragm, receiving sunlight and moonlight.
Galaxies and nebulae talk to you, comets sing,
you wear rainbows as a necklace.

The attrition of wind and rain
fails to erode your silent majesty.
Archaeologists and anthropologists
conjecture on your meaning,
but to me it is enhanced
by subjectivity; my finitude
besides your longevity,
a sense of numinous awe,
the dwindling to a pinprick
of my own significance.

My visits to you therefore
stand as pilgrimages, whether
through cloisters of clouds,
vast halls of mist. Cloaked in
remoteness, you play hide and seek
with the contours, the swivelling light.
I like it best in May, when you dwell
within the blandishments of Spring.
Resting against your orthostat,

a diva skylark sings for me,
Whitethorn burns its incense and
from somewhere in the dark forest,
that African visitor casts
his two note spell over
your nonchalant, granite grin.

PRIMROSES

bypassed by the muses of Spring
they huddle in clusters
along hedgerows   river banks
untrodden places
for primroses are introvert
self-contained   they have no truck
with their gawdy cousins
they do not march as golden hosts
nor troop their own colour
they do not belong to architects
town planners   garden centres
pale and lemony   timorous
yet robust   they listen to Radio Three
and write poetry   scribbling lines
on their green striated leaves
soft as lamb's ears
if you care to linger
lower your head   their scent
more delicate and memorable
than the best Chanel

this time of year,
if you pass through
Glenballyemon   Glendun
Cregagh Forest   where
the woodpecker drills
they have peppered
for endless miles
the verges and hedgerows
their petaline beauty glittering
like Van Gogh's chandeliered stars

SWALLOWS, AN ADDENDUM.

I told you before about the swallows,
the frenetic, frenzied zig-zag of their flight,
the Heathrow they maintained
in the old byre, their pimpled nests
adhering to the rafters like clams.
But this is September and they have sensed
an equinox approaching, an equatorial pull,
so now they are gone. If they arrived
as the gift wrapping of spring,
they are gone in the mournful wake
for summer, leaving a tangible silence;
the buildings they once invigorated,
deserted as a famine village.

Yet there must be a somewhere
their flight still delights.
As the muezzin drifts from tall minarets,
they weave across elephant grass,
Saharan dust still in their wings.

Geraldine Fleming

Born and raised in Northern Ireland, Geraldine Fleming had an all-consuming career in Social Work. Feeling bereft of purpose when ill health forced early retirement, she found herself drawn into the world of creative writing. She is a member of North Coast Writers and Ballymoney Writers Groups.

Her prose and poetry appear in a number of anthologies and journals. Recently several short stories have been published in four anthologies New Worlds New Voices, Ulster University Press, and in Love, Loss and Cardiac Issues, Irish Hares and Sea Horses, and Spun Yarns and Woven Words, all three published by Impspired Press. In 2022, two poems were published in the Community Arts Partnership Anthology, Threshold and her poem cartographer was long listed for the Seamus Heaney Award.

In 2023, her first collection of short stories, Curiosity, was published, closely followed by her first poetry collection, Fractured Echoes, both by Impspired Press.

a rediscovered land

trekking uneven terrain   tramping clots of bogland
lower hills consumed by sturdy strides
whipping winds strive to petrify my very bones
calcify me into infinity

below the crust deep veins transverse time
Palaeozoic rocks tumble their way into every present day
while famine walls weave mycorrhizal networks
rasping ideas of   equality   freedom   forgiveness

above   a skylark rapt in an aerial aria
trills & tootles his unique song
i try to keep the fleeting blip in focus
passing the ridge he is sky-eaten

ahead is a spinney   pricked by gaunt pillars of light
ancient ghosts flicker & flit content in their gloom
suspicion of the summit breaks a grey mutinous skyline
a mirage   merely a crag cloaked in trickster mist
teasing vision   another summit rests higher   beyond
& beyond again   a roll of ridged creases

i arrive at my own meridian   in the stillness
Muninn & Huginn   whispering ravens
strong of wing & sharp of beak
return to perch   relaying thoughts & memories

night driving

scrunched nose to the windscreen
rookie grey knuckles welded at nine and three
fugitive rain-rods of night silver coruscate
in the high beam

shunted by wintered mountain squalls   along
a slither of drenched   puddle-riddled road
sour whiskey and bakery whites choke the heated air
he sleeps beside you

8 track Patsy falls to pieces again   challenged
by the clicking rosary beads and
muttered devotions from the back seat
she rocks behind you

within the bright arc tousled whins fringe
guzzling ditches   beyond in the void
a torch light flinches twice then dies
you join the solo prayer

grip tighter
                    sit straighter
                                        breath deeper

Saturday wages paid for your haircut
at a legal check point   would you look older
older than fourteen   no choice
you continue driving home

                                        decompression arrives years later

A Slice of Soda

Shirley relaxed her shoulders just enough to remove her kid gloves and stow them in the crocodile handbag braced in the crook of her arm. Curling her fingers around the shiny brass knocker she gave two brisk taps on the over-painted door. Fibres from a recent encounter with Brasso gritted her fingers, clinging to her red nail polish. She almost tutted as she snapped the clasp on her bag, the clatter returned her to the morning's task.

So far not one furtive net curtain had noted her arrival. She had parked on the main road and walked through the tight hodgepodge of streets to the address, 79 Warnock Street. A cold wind whipped along the narrow street catching barely a single fragment of dust to reward its effort. Shuddering she rapped the knocker again, harder.

That morning she hadn't eaten breakfast. Instead, she carefully chose her outfit. A fitted maroon two-piece suit teamed with a camel swing back coat. She had taken special care with her make-up too, the expensive pressed powder hid sunken dark hollows under her hazel eyes. Covered her exhaustion.

Still, no one answered the door. She could feel her plan unravelling much like her courage.

Just one more time, then if there's no answer- if there's no answer I'll just have to come back later.

Leaning forward she made a fist and hammered the door three times.

Well, if there's someone home, they'll have heard that-whole bloody street probably did.

Shirley held her breath, listening for the sound of a bolt drawing back or a neighbour asking what she wanted. Nothing happened. Just as she was about to leave, she heard the slow scrape of a lock turning. As the door opened, she rehearsed her speech. One delivered so many times before. At so many houses and flats on so many streets, to so many women.

How many times now... exactly? She asked herself.

Why pretend you can't remember. This brings it into double figures.

She swallowed the rising bile, breathed hard through her mouth and prepared to greet the occupant. A small plump, red cheeked woman stood in the doorway. She wore a nylon apron over her floral blouse and black skirt. With grey hair still in curlers and bound in a pink hair net she resembled a little Russian doll. Shirley stood open mouthed, she could not speak a word.

'Yes dear, can I help you? Have you been knocking long?'

'Sorry to disturb you, I'm looking for Sheila.'

'Yes dear.' Looking down she wiped her hands on the apron.

'Now if it's insurance, I don't want any. And I'm not one for buying anything on tick if that's what you're about.'

For the first time Shirley's lines didn't fit this scenario.

'No, nothing like that Sheila, may I call you Sheila?

At that moment another cutting blast of wind raged the length of the street and Shirley shivered.

'Look it's cold, you're freezing there. You're nearly blue. Come in … as long as you're not selling anything?'

'No, I promise I'm not selling anything.'

***

Sheila opened the door wider. Looking over her shoulder she led the way along the narrow hall. The house seemed familiar. Shirley drifted toward memories she felt belonged to someone else. She could feel the swing of girlish white-socked legs, tap impatiently against a chair runner waiting for soda bread to be delivered from her grandmother's range.

Sheila turned off the radio.

'Sorry I like to get the morning news. The world these days … well what can you say.'

Sheila shook her head of curlers as if to dislodge an annoying thought. The table had rings of flour and sticky baking debris.

'It's warmer in the kitchen. I'm just baking soda bread. Have a seat and I'll get us a cuppa. Get you warmed up. I keep meaning to get one of those new ding dong bells, I don't think there is a lot of point now.'

She busied herself with tea making. Giving the younger woman time to settle. The smell of fresh bread lit up the kitchen. Resurrecting long lost hopes and dreams.

'You're baking.' Finally, she found something to say.

'Yes, usually I bake on a Tuesday but I've a hospital appointment tomorrow so it's all a bit of a rush. But I've it finished now.'

Setting two china cups and a steaming teapot on the table Sheila sat down with Shirley, one at either end of the now immaculate table.

For the first time they openly studied each other, Grand Masters deciding on their next moves. Shirley didn't think she could trust herself to talk without crying. The unexpected situation, the force of memories disarmed her usual staid presence. She lifted the tea and began to sip. It was strong and sweet, she hadn't noticed the milk and sugar going in but it was like nectar to her. The reviver began to thread its way toward a deep coldness. Sheila held the silence a little longer.

'How are you now? she ventured. 'Thawing out, I hope. This road is the coldest place on earth. I wouldn't be surprised if an iceberg floated past my door.'

Catching Shirley's eye, she held it for just one moment longer than necessary.

'Well now, I think you were about to tell me your name. Oh, would you like a slice? I think we could risk a round with butter and jam.' Sheila nodded in the direction of two bumps of loaves draped with linen towels.

'Yes please, that sounds lovely. I'm Shirley... Shirley Longshaw.'

She stretched out her hand just as Sheila set the fresh bread slathered in butter and jam on the table.

'Pleased to meet you, Shirley.'

Their hands clasped, as different from one another as they could be. One manicured, soft and delicate, the other strengthened by hard work and gnarled by years. A gentle vitality flowed from one to the other.

'Eat up Shirley and then you can tell me what it's all about.'

'I came here to talk to a woman called Sheila, a woman I believe my husband is seeing. I came to ask her to stop the affair.'

She had voiced her petition yet she was sure Sheila was not the other woman. The others were always younger, prettier, looking for something, true love, a helping hand in their career, or just a good time, dancing, holidays, gifts. She had an approach for each type once she knew their motivation. If a heavy dose of guilt or shame didn't work, she found the money in the white envelope in her bag was a winner- break it off now!

In the kitchen oasis the ticking clock held the heartbeat of their existence. Sheila watched the younger woman's conflicts tumble, like shafts on a lock against the wrong key.

'You know I am not the other woman. I've known other women but never been one. This is not the first time you have intervened, is it?'

They had moved to sit in fireside chairs either side of the range. Both nursed their teacups. Shirley traced the tiny flower pattern around the china cup, watching the darkness of her shadow-finger. There was only tenderness in the other's face. No reproach, or disgust or shame. With shock she realised those devils just lived inside of her. Tormenting her.

'Yes, I know that. I was the other woman once. I'm... I'm paying for past pain I caused. I met him when I was eighteen, he came to work for my father. He was married, I knew that. I'm thirty-two tomorrow. This is the tenth time I have come to speak to the other woman.'

She wanted to hang her head in disgrace but Sheila's presence seemed to hold her firm in the orbit of the room.

'Ten you say... What a busy man Mr Longshaw is. Do you think he'll ever stop?'

The question hung like a banner strung across the hearth. She had never considered this before. Always the effort was locate and defuse, like dealing with an unexploded bomb.

'Busy... yes. Practically one a year... that I know about. Do... do you think he will stop? He's bound to just settle soon... isn't he?'

Despite the plea in her voice Sheila could not lie.

'It'd be wrong of me to tell you just what you want to hear. 'Specially when you already know the truth, in your heart. You've always known really.'

Shirley's emotions flooded over in the starkness of a home truth. She wept. She wept long and hard for lost years, for twisted devotion and vain hope that things would change, that he would change. She wept for lost opportunities and the guilt she carried. She cried for all the maybes', maybe if they had children, maybe if he hadn't been successful, maybe if they lived in a different town, if she was prettier, funnier, sexier, taller, smaller. As the list gathered speed the absurdity of it all struck her. All through the outpouring the steady strong arm rested around her shoulder and smuggled in hankies through the gaps in wails and blubbers. Sheila never muttered don't cry or tried to stem the flow, she understood it had to be excised. The wound was laid bare and the salt, now stinging would later cleanse.

Eventually, a steadiness came over Shirley, part exhaustion, mostly relief. Within the haven of the small room barriers dissolved. Fortified by memories of long-ago slices shared, and an encounter with a stranger a new kind of understanding took seed.

'Sorry … I have never been like this. I really ought to be embarrassed but oddly I'm not.'

'Nothing to be apologising for. I think you need another cuppa, I know I certainly do.'

Again, she busied with the tea making. This time she placed two large mugs on the edge of the range.

'If I had whisky, I would put a tot in but I'm not a drinker so extra sugar will have to do the job.' She lifted her mug as if to toast the event.

A sudden thought occurred to Shirley.

'Is your name really Sheila?'

'No... well you have me there. Sheila lives 79 Warnock Street, this is 79 Warnock Road. She is two streets over and one up.'

'I don't understand. Why'd you say yes when I asked at the door?'

'Truth be told, Shirley, only desperate wives look for Sheila. She likes married men. Likes to humiliate the wives who come to her door. I just thought I could save you that. I'm sorry I just did it on the spur. I'm Bella, that's my name... Bella Hope.

***

In the silence, broken only by the coals in the fire rearranging themselves Bella flicked breadcrumbs of her apron. Allowing a long-held secret to surface she spoke in a whisper.

'She makes a game of it you know. Who she can entrap, who will come to plead for their husband back. She was nineteen and just testing her power over men. The Catherine Wheel burns bright and fast. I just let it run its course. I forgave him.'

'God, Bella.'

Shirley leaned over and squeezed her hand. Bella mopped tears with the corner of her apron and smiled. Shirley understood this was not pain but sadness. They sat at ease listening to the pings of the cooling oven and the ticking clock, each deep in thought. Though not dissimilar thoughts.

'I think he is like that too you know. Leaving trails for me to follow. It's a game to him too. But this is not a game for me, not any longer. I'm not a piece on a chess board.'

***

Long past lunchtime the door to 79 Warnock Road opened. Shirley's face, free of the remains of her tormented make-up, shone in winter sun.

'I'll call over at nine in the morning. We will go to the hospital together... And please Bella... answer the door.'

Arc of the Sun

dawn's eternal creep
ruptures the horizon
prepares the way for its savage soaring glare
builds to a crescendo by midday   midway

launches seeds of superheated air
pops and puffs out desiccated lungs
melts glaciers and simmers seas
in summer transit   first blush to dusk

when fists of lumens pummel retinas
we squint and peep from shaded eyes
at scorched lands and ravaged futures
belying wonderment and fear   so bittersweet

pulling flimsy curtains taut then tighter
ghosting humanity's survival
oblivious to our planetary distress
repressing sound conclusions   filthy lucre over life

industrialised legacy soars and earth becomes a husk
purge your apathy as nadir edges closer
uncover your denial
discover your fight   now

A Good Fermanagh Man

The ladies of the parish had rallied together to cater for Dominic McCarthy's wake. It was going to be a big funeral, industrial geysers and bucket sized teapots were shipped in by Coulter's lorry along with six dozen chairs and a garden marquee from the parish hall. Dominic, God rest his soul, had been a quiet man, a family man, a good Mass goer who handed over his envelope each Sunday. Strangely though that wasn't the reason for the flurry of Vatican scale activity. His son, Nick was expected home. Jetting in from Hollywood the action star, Shakespearean actor and latterly director, was central to this production. The ladies fair clucked and chuckled in anticipation, hormone patches were applied with extra care.

'Of course, he would be home for his father's wake. Thon place wouldn't change a good Fermanagh man.'

Breda blurted, a spray of cake crumbs almost breaking the speed limit. The naysayer hung her head in shame for suggesting he might be too busy.

Dymphna, quiet for once, thanked her nervous stomach for keeping her tongue still. Slow swipes of the tea towel around the mishmash of side plates wound her fantasies toward reality.

I'll get to see him in the actual flesh. Breathe the same air... Oh my God is this bad of me? Am I destined for hell? What would PJ say?

The clink of china on her wedding band bombed PJ into the mix, dampening expectations, but only for a moment.

This is meant to be... it's just meant to be... Became her heart song.

She hadn't grown up with him like the other women, still a blow-in after twenty years. She watched as each in turn went to the bathroom to check make-up and redo lipstick. Hair by Miriam had opened at seven to cope with the unexpected rush. Miriam had apologised, she just couldn't fit Dymphna in for a wash and blow-dry before she was due to join the tea rota at the wake house.

'Sorry, no can do. I can fit you in next Wednesday. How does that suit?' She chirped like a budgie on the line.

Dymphna had done the best she could with her fine brown hair scooping it into a pony tail. Palming her lipstick and compact she snuck out to the backyard and leaned against the coal shed.

Just keep cool, keep cool was added to the litany spooling in her head. She had just taken the top off her Red Diva lipstick when the sound of slow crunching steps on the back lane provoked a glance in that direction. There he was, all six foot two of him, shoulders like a barn door, hands clasped behind his back and trademark unruly auburn hair, all his own too. No bodyguards. Just him, studying his own footfall. Retracing steps he must have taken a thousand times. Her breath left her, the air around her thinned and her body swayed like a reed by the lough side.

Before she could step forward, as she had just instructed her legs to do, the coven descended like a plague of long-lost sisters. In the scrum to welcome him to his sadness she was all but pitched behind the shed. She straightened herself, for no other hand would help her and soothed her pride with the assurance no one had noticed – Thank God.

***

They surrounded him like insulating foam, no space left unfilled and moved indoors. Words of condolence stood incongruous with the too-long hugs and pouting smiles. Breda, being the boldest and claiming to know him the best had most to prove to the entourage. She smoothed the material of his suit sleeves, everyone present was hypnotised by her tiger strip and diamante manicure. And with eyes like crocus bulbs yearning for spring she stared up square into Nick's face and purred.

'What a lovely suit Nick. Your dad would be proud. Did you get it special?'

Dymphna couldn't hear the reply, his voice was low and there was a backwash of chatter. Blithely Breda linked his arm like bride and groom after the event, leading him into the wake room. Still welded to his side she leaned in almost resting her head on him.

'Sure, aren't we the same now Nick, both only orphans. Your wee mammy away this five years and now your daddy lying there.' She sniffed, for effect. 'But doesn't he look well. O' Kane's do a great job, very professional. Their son Cahal did make-up for the Game of Thrones. You weren't in that were you?'

Nick didn't answer that directly, Dymphna doubted he even heard it. Instead, he turned around, one hand resting on the coffin and spoke to them all. She saw how his face was etched with loss and his voice struggled to compose a few words.

'I expect there'll be a lot of people here today. My father was a popular man, devoted to the parish. Before people start to arrive, I would appreciate some time on my own with him. Thank you all for your help, I appreciate it very much, we both do.'

Just as he turned back to the coffin, to his father, Breda chirped up on behalf of the clique.

'Of course ... of course Nick, we have things to be getting on with. But I think a decade of the Rosary is called for. Your father would expect it. He was a desperate man for the Rosary.'

Like a master magician she produced a set of beads, launching the decade into full murmuring swing. Dymphna watched as he held his father's hand. She didn't think she had ever seen someone look so alone in a shoulder-to-shoulder room as Nick McCarthy at that moment.

All five foot two of Breda could easily pass as a regular for the Stasi with sergeant stripes included. Even the men at the bottom of the road directing traffic and holding back reporters crumpled under her gaze. A quiet word from her had reduced several people to tatters. She assigned roles and Dymphna was dish collection and washing up. After school got out a few of the youngsters came over to help her, she was glad of that. It was an invisible job, mostly elbow deep in soap suds. The slow swipe had given way to a wide handed drag front and back before setting up for the servers again.

Snippets of gossip, like stage whispers, blabbed their way around the kitchen. Private exchanges earwigged by the flittering wake servers were repeated. The arrival of Eddie, Dominic's bowls partner proved fodder for Breda and her haughty hiss.

'God help him. Says he'll not sleep tonight, nor does he want to. He wishes he had more time with his father. Your heart bleeds for him. Sure, don't we all wish for that. Longs to hear him play his fiddle by the glow of the range and walk through lanes as seasons turn, blethering their way along. Very poetic... I'm sure he'll speak lovely at the funeral.'

Dymphna imagined how his day passed in a blur of pressed hands, slow nods and an ear to distant guffaws from the yarning corners.

The garden marquee hadn't stopped all day. It was like a holding pattern for people coming into land in the wake room and then taxiing to another area to load again with refreshments before taking off. PJ called in after work but she hadn't time to speak other than arrange he would pick her up when she was ready. By eleven o'clock the last stragglers had found their manners and gone home. Before the servers decanted to the parish hall to do the prep work for day two, Breda mustered them in her team talk.

'We've to get ahead of the curve here ladies. You think it was bad today, tomorrow will be worse. Let's get to it.'

Dymphna heard a few whimpers and resolutions to wear flat shoes tomorrow. There was an unidentified 'every dog has it's day' comment but in the interest of self-preservation everyone pretended they hadn't heard it. With two sharp claps she dismissed them.

***

One final sweep around for stray dishes should do it. In the calmness she decided to leave the wake room 'til last. A light tap on the door and she stepped inside. Nick sat alone, his chair dragged as close as possible to his father. He lifted his head from his hands and scooped away the tears from his face. His shoulders, broad as they were, heaved with grief.

'It's Dymphna, isn't it?' he tried to smile, to brighten himself.

'Yes, that's right Nick.' She pulled a crumpled tissue from her pocket and passed it to him, a sign of no intrusion.

'It's clean.' she assured him. Uncertain of what to say or do she bit her lip.

'I'll miss Dominic. Your mammy and him were so good to me from I arrived here. Like family.'

'He often mentioned you, was very fond of you too. Said mammy and him always said if they had a daughter, she'd be just like you.' He drew himself straight in the chair, unashamed of his tears.

'You know they were pleased as punch for you. Proud of your achievements. I probably know more about you than you would believe. They were full of stories and every mention, every review was snipped out and put in 'Nick's Book' as they called it. It's safe, by the way, sitting in the bottom of your mammy's wardrobe...things could grow legs here, you know yourself how it is.'

She held her hands behind her back in much the same pensive manner he had earlier and listened.

'I wonder, Dymphna if I did enough for them? I'm sure having no brothers or sisters made my choices harder on them. Hard on me too. They were determined not to leave here. Kept telling me about their roots. And you and PJ – always so good. It was as much as I could do to get them to come to me for the winter months...That's all gone now...'

He looked up into her face, searching for answers to unknowables. The person she had conjured from the big screen was only a fiction, an image of someone else's creation. The man, now just a man, devoid of lights and lines and clever editing was cast on the shores of regret wading in the shallows of 'how will I go on.' She could see ripples of pain and loss radiate around him.

'They were a darlin' couple and we had great times together. They'll leave a big gap, that's for sure. They wouldn't have had it any other way for you. And God Nick, in those months each year youse saw more of each other than

PJ sees his mammy and sure she's only the next field over from us. Life takes over, we all know that. Your mammy always said 'so long as Nick is happy that's all we need.' It was that simple and that true.'

He nodded, that slow nod when you know something is essentially right but need time to cultivate the seeds of understanding. He patted the seat near him.

'Care for a seat? You must be exhausted. That Breda is some task master, isn't she? She would do well managing some of the production companies in Hollywood.' They both smiled and sat in an easy silence.

'Can I get you anything before I go? PJ will be calling over for me soon.'

'Let's have a cup of tea together. I'm parched. Are there any Jammie Dodgers left, I'm partial to them.'

Two cups of tea, half a packet of biscuits and a chat on the phone with PJ, Nick had decided to move one of the good chairs into the room so he could spend the night with his father and Dymphna had fished out his mammy's knee rug for him.

'They will both be here with you now.' she unfolded the lilac knitted blanket as she walked back into the room. Each square had a different pattern, all drawn together into one.

'I'm looking forward to seeing PJ again. Good of him to say he'd sit with me a while tonight- a good lad. You know Dymphna, PJ and me were in the same class...I'm sure he's said... growing up we did everything together. When I went away I … I wasn't good at keeping in touch. My bad as they say. Have to tell you though I think he is a lucky man.'

***

The latch on the back door clicked. At the sound of familiar steps Dymphna felt her heart leap, her earlier confusion long evaporated. She smiled. PJ, with a grace you couldn't expect from a man his height, shook hands with Nick and settled on the chair next to her, instinctively they reached for each other's hand. He touched the coffin, his blue eyes filled with tears.

'Awh Nick there just aren't the words are there? I'm so sad. Your father … he'll always be with us, in our hearts.'

'PJ it's so good to see you. Could be better circumstances... yes but you'd nearly think he organised it this way. He always was a wily man. He was always one step ahead of us.'

'Never a truer word. And we hadn't a baldy notion he was on our case.' He tapped the old photo albums he had set on the floor.

'Love, me and Nick are going to relive our glory days, there are pictures in here of Dominic in full flow -on the fiddle too.'

'Everything's grand at home. The boys are with me mammy. Take you your coat and head home for a rest. You look like you've been Breda-ed.'

The three of them laughed. Going over to say goodnight to Dominic she fancied she saw a little roguish grin fleet across his face. She paused, the entirety of the day running through her mind. Like soap bubbles swirling down the drain, she had rinsed away the fantasy and allowed herself to feel the loss of her good friend.

Sinead Coxhill

Having grown up on a farm in Northern Ireland, Sinéad Coxhill studied English at Queen's University Belfast before moving to England where she lived on a smallholding in Suffolk with her now ex-husband, rearing rare breed pigs and growing their own vegetables. Returning to Northern Ireland in 2013, she settled in the north coast town of Portrush, where she began writing poetry in 2014, joining Portrush Writers and later, North Coast Writers.

Her poem *Milking Time* was selected by Waterstones, Coleraine, Northern Ireland, as part of a month-long display of poems for International Women's Day in 2016. Touring parts of England performing at open mic events in 2018, the following year she performed at Waterstones in Birmingham as part of a group of English and Northern Irish poets. Also in 2019, she performed at the Red Sails and Stendhal Festivals, in 2022 at the Abbey Lane Theatre, Armagh, and in 2023 at the Swell festival in Portrush, all in Northern Ireland. In 2022 she won a bursary to attend the John Hewitt Literary Arts Festival and Summer School in Armagh.

Her poems have been published in 8 anthologies: *Spindrift,* Portrush Writers, 2018, the Community Arts Partnership anthology *Heartland,* 2020, *Reeling In,* Portrush Writers, 2021, *Irish Hares and Seahorses,* a North Coast Writers anthology, Impspired Press, 2022, *Across the Threshold,* a pamphlet and companion publication to the Community Arts Partnership's Threshold anthology, 2022, *Love Loss and Cardiac Matters,* Impspired Press, 2022, *Compass,* a Community Arts Partnership anthology, 2023, *Spun Yarns and Woven Words,* Impspired Press, 2023.

In September 2023 her debut Poetry Collection, *Menopausal Mermaids and Life Lines* was published by Impspired Press.

I Come From

(after Robert Seatter)

I come from hay fields
with fragrant meadow sweet
and curlew call
from the Moss
where the turf is cut
curing in the sunshine
and summer breeze

I come from Belfast
I come from care-free
student days
enjoying the craic
in the Empire Bar
Lavery's and the Limelight
sharing a flat with friends
bantering over who uses
the most electricity

I come from Stanstead in Suffolk
from walks in barley and rape fields
enjoying the shade of woods
in the heat of the summer
listening out for the nightingale

I come from the sea
from icy dips
and walks on the shore
drinking sights and sounds
writing down sensations

December Sunset

clouds suffused in tangerine
a December sunset
in all its ostentation

pink tipped waves
seduce sand
a spectacle   a drama

I file the images with care
wanting home to write them
but arrested by fading hues

my memory clings to tendrils
of a shade shifting picture

mourning the gap between
what I see and what I write

January Sunset

an infusion of mist
and spindrift
mystical white swirl
with gilded splash
of sunset
dappling the water

waves bless the shore
walkers smile
~ stopping ~
to drink in
the quiescence
souls renewed

Midnight

midnight sounds its sonorous bell

indigo skies cast a long shadow

darkness envelops

night falling softly

in sombre shade

gracing the penumbra

holding day to ransom

the dawn will approach

'An acrostic is a piece of writing in which a particular set of letters – typically the first letter of each line, word or paragraph – spells out a word or phrase with special significance to the text.'

Springboards : A Creative Writing Manual, Mary Farrell, Impspired, 2022

Seascapes

the sea in its palette of greens
is painted into my memory

shucking of lapping waters
over pebbles and shells

waves glide   formation dancers
seaweed strewn   cassette ribbons

a solitary beach walk
but never really alone

vertiginous waters   lowering sky
sudden downpour scours breakers
each is rinsed   renewed

I open my lips
swallow wind and rain
to experience all inside me

Deserted

storms come
without witness
violent beyond
our endurance
Sea must struggle

alone

suffering unwitnessed
unacknowledged
a lonely time for her
powerful but isolated
strong but disregarded

physically full of fire
and energy
but emotionally
depleted
deserted

Jeremiah Flies High

1.

Jeremiah loved his home. He snuggled down under his moss coverlet, revelling in its woodland scent and softness. He smiled towards the sticky weed he'd found while walking in the woods. Luckily he'd owned a sturdy silver thimble and used it to pot his 'plant'. Jeremiah liked its stickiness. It made him think of something a traveller might have found in the Tropics. A desire to travel and see the world burned brightly in him.

New construction projects swam through his thoughts. He'd recently moved from his rickety, old glass house to the newly empty badger's sett. The first chamber of the sett contained his living room and bedroom. Cynthia, the vole and Belinda, the dormouse each had a chamber in the sett as well. Cynthia had a very small living room and bedroom. Most of the space was given over to a recording studio for her singing. Belinda had a tiny bedroom. The rest of the space was her kitchen. She loved baking and cooking. She particularly enjoyed feeding Jeremiah when he was absorbed in one of his projects and forgot all about eating.

He'd decided to make his bedroom smaller so that he could create a workshop for himself. Recently, while walking he'd found a sycamore seed. It was the perfect propeller. Jeremiah was good with his hands. He was convinced that with ingenuity and endeavour it would be possible to create his own helicopter. It would take time, patience and a lot of foraging to get the things needed for the project.

The disused toy factory, that was where treasures might be discovered. Jeremiah made frequent trips there, always coming back loaded down and happy. One day it was a wind shield from a child's toy car, on another, seats from a miniature land rover.

Often the sound of hammering from his workshop competed with the music of Cynthia singing her scales. Belinda cooked happily, loving the liveliness of their home.

Finally the helicopter was built. Jeremiah decided that Belinda and Cynthia should be his first passengers. Belinda had cooked delicious meals for him while he worked. All the noise he'd made had been tolerated by Cynthia.

2.

The helicopter made a put-put noise as it rose into the air. Jeremiah was alarmed when almost immediately it began dropping downwards. He pulled hard on the joystick and thankfully the helicopter began to steadily climb. He breathed freely again and smiled.

Belinda and Cynthia hugged each other in glee as it rose up over the river. They watched the fishermen and barges become smaller and smaller. As the helicopter flew over the village, they all saw the villagers comings and goings. Cynthia admired the neat vegetable gardens. Belinda expressed her delight in the loveliness of the church with the sun shining on its spire. She had never before appreciated how beautifully it was made.

They continued onward over the small wood, watching two little elves playing chase among the trees. Running very fast, suddenly one tripped and went sprawling on the ground. He lay still and his friend called his name urgently.

Basil are you OK? Talk to me.

Jeremiah knew that it wouldn't be safe to try and land among the trees. Luckily they were almost at the edge of the wood with a meadow just beyond. He flew towards it and landed within minutes. Together with Cynthia and Belinda he rushed towards the two little elves.

Basil was now sitting at the base of a tree, looking very sorry for himself. His tear stained face was muddy and both his knees were cut. Belinda took charge, lifting her satchel from her shoulder. She always carried it in case of an emergency. Taking out a bottle of witch hazel and bandages, she began to clean and bandage Basil's knees. Luckily he didn't appear to have suffered any other injuries.

The other little chap was called Cyril. He approached Jeremiah half boldly, half shyly.

Can you fly us home 'cos Basil's hurt?

Jeremiah nodded and smiled.

Of course. I don't want him to have to struggle with his injured knees.

Cyril jumped up and down cheering. Basil looked happier. Jeremiah scratched his chin. He was thinking it was going to be a bit of a squeeze with all of them in the helicopter. A few minutes later they piled into the cockpit... all fitting in. It was as if the little helicopter breathed out to allow them a bit more space. Soon Cyril, all shyness gone was chatting eagerly to Jeremiah, directing him to where he and Basil lived. He pointed out an abandoned, tumble down farm. Jeremiah had a bird's eye view of dilapidated sheds, barns and outhouses. Two disused hen houses were home to Cyril and Basil's families.

Jeremiah landed the helicopter a short distance from the hen houses. Seconds later four elves came rushing out. Introducing themselves as Basil and Cyril's parents. When they learnt of the accident they clapped Jeremiah warmly on the back and said they couldn't thank him enough for bringing the boys safely home. They thanked Belinda and Cynthia also.

The happy elves gathered round to admire the helicopter, saying how well constructed it was. Jeremiah blushed and smiled modestly. A slight distance from everyone, the two mothers had been engaged in a lively chat. They now announced that they wanted to invite Jeremiah and his friends to a party on Sunday. Since sharing the badger's sett with Belinda and Cynthia, Jeremiah was less shy and happily agreed to come. After making promises to meet up, Jeremiah, Cynthia and Belinda took off in the helicopter once again.

3.

The following week, Jeremiah took his brothers up in his helicopter. They had persuaded him into carrying out a dawn flight. They wanted to watch the sun coming up. Jeremiah and his three brothers chatted excitedly. Passing over the woods, the tree tops were bathed in a soft light. The clouds were a glorious pink. Soon they reached the river. With the rising sun shining on it, it was a spool of gold rolling its way through the countryside.

Keen eyed Jeremiah, spotted a frail elderly elf walking slowly by the riverside. He was wearing pyjamas and a dressing gown. Jeremiah recognised him from last week's party as Cyril's grandfather, Cuthbert.

I wonder if he's sleepwalking? I may need to get him back home to his family,

Jeremiah spoke to his brothers. He focused on landing the helicopter at a slight distance from Cuthbert not to startle him.

The four elves climbed out of the helicopter. Jack suggested that Jeremiah should approach Cuthbert on his own. He was concerned that the sight of three strange faces might make Cuthbert anxious. Jeremiah walked slowly and quietly towards him. A weak voice called out.

Who's there? Where am I?

It's me, Jeremiah.

Speaking gently, he put a reassuring hand on Cuthbert's arm. He explained that he thought Cuthbert had been sleep walking and had probably left his house in the early hours of the morning.

Don’t worry, I can get you home in the helicopter in a few minutes.

Cuthbert seemed a little happier now. Jeremiah beckoned over his brothers to introduce them to each other. As they flew the short distance to Cuthbert’s home, Jeremiah’s brothers couldn’t help noticing that he kept grinning to himself. He could scarcely contain his excitement. He was enjoying a wonderful day dream of working as a Search and Rescue pilot. He resolved to make his dream come true.

Mae Gardiner

Living on the North Coast of Ireland, Mae Gardiner draws inspiration from the people and places around her. She writes children's fairy tales, poetry, short stories and also paints. Having performed at Atlantic Craft NI Events throughout Ireland, her 'A Coat of Many Colours', 2020, is available on YouTube. Many of her poems were first published in three Anthologies from Portrush Writers Group, Beachcombing 2014, Spindrift 2018 and Reeling In 2021. Three of her pieces featured in both the Anthologies by North Coast Writers, Irish Hares and Seahorses 2022, and Spun Tales and Woven Words 2023, and her poem Not just yet featured in the Anthology Love, Loss and Cardiac Issues, all of which were published by Impspired Press in 2022.

The Bathtub

The moonlight taps the windowpane above my head while the sweet smell of neroli penetrates the bedroom and fills my mind with sadness. The puffed-up pillows hold the weight of my spine. A soft cotton sheet wraps my legs in whitewash. A pink glittery diary, blunt pencil and a rubber are tied together with an elastic band on the bedside table. The novel is on the bed as I pretend to read.

The door is open halfway between the messy bedroom and the ensuite. Hot water runs steadily while the vapour interrupts my thoughts, casting a fog on the day's events. I watch him carefully. Tossing his clothing into a heap on the floor he stands for a few moments arranging towels and a fluffy mat. The angry scars run from the highest point of his upper arm and end at his wrist suddenly. Like a crossword puzzle they appear horizontal across the hip, make a sharp right angle, and continue downwards to the ankle. After all these years the stitching still has a Frankenstein effect, they remain raised and irritate him.

Stepping into the bath slowly, methodically he lies back fully, embracing the fizz of the bubbles, he immerses his head for a few seconds before he comes up for air. The condensation continues to waft and blow behind the door. It blocks my view. In silence I pull it open further with my foot. Under the glare of a hard lit mirror, I watch as he submerges his weary body yet again, leaving only his nostrils to gasp the air. The plumbing creaks as I eavesdrop on his deep sighing. His chest rises and falls. I can see his blood pressure increase with the temperature of the bath water as his face reddens to the colour of a ripe beetroot. The smell of Lavender oil leaks from a bar of half used soap hiding beneath a white cotton cloth. He grabs both and slathering the cloth with several wipes of the soap he scrubs the remnants of pain from his face. His eyes sting but he continues to scour his brow and slaps the rag into the water afterwards. It clings to his torso like an old plastic bag you might see stuck in a hedge. Carelessly he reaches for a large tub of own brand supermarket shampoo and knocks the conditioner into the bath beside him tutting. He slarries his hands with enough liquid from the bottle to wash several children, slaps it on his head and beard, then lathers it so long it resembles a small cloud.

I open the door, step in carrying the weight of my words. Pain and loss bruise my soul as I flip the lid of the toilet seat down and sit on its cold, welcome knee. Thoughts pierce my consciousness. Tears slide down my face, plop off the edge of my cheeks. For the first time I noticed a single freckle on his ring finger just above the gold wedding band. "Is it that date already?". I nod and he reaches across, pushes the frizzy hair that licks the side of my face. I pretend to smile. A single slick smudge of oil creeps across the brink of the steel handle and clings to it stubbornly. He pulls me forwards and kisses me while the water clinks, smacks over the sides of the enamel. I can't help looking at the mess that slurps down the floor tiles like an unruly stream. Tasting salty oil and soap on emery board lips I pick the old skin with the edge of my tooth and swallow it. The tap continues to drip. Steam runs down the wall tiles in a zigzag motion. Reaching forwards, he pulls out the hefty plughole. The bath groans at the sudden force rattling down its inners. I watch the soap suds play tig and chase each other merrily down the drain as he stands up, wraps himself in a large white towel and pads out with a squelching noise.

The bath has a dark tidemark gleaned into its otherwise white interior. I wonder how many mothers, fathers and children have plunged their faces in here before we moved in. I can see my reflection mirrored in the foggy glass window but when I lean forwards to examine my eyes an old woman with wiry red hair looks at me, so I retreat to the bedroom. The pillows and freshly laundered sheets are strewn across the base of the bed. He lies on his side already half asleep.

The Enigmatic Elf

~ written on the day of my grandson Ryan's birth ~

North Wind appeared in a blizzard vapour
filled with grey anger he had a passion
with no explanation   vexation with no translation
he sought her out
believing he could catch her
in his storm clouds

she was a mere fairy   many realms beneath him
living in a magic well deep in Norwegian countryside
in a faraway myth
in a land where Legends were facts
where people revere fairies
fed goblins   even dedicated trees
to all the tiny spirits
protecting them
so North Wind would
never
find the pixie people

he blasted down through each cloud
piercing their skin with his sharp nails
each cloud lacerated
raining down on those far below
he whisked up a typhoon
sending it before him
laughing at his own ferocity
even more determined to seize his prize

Enigmatic Elf
held the power to change
the direction he would blow
if he had her held high
above the earthly realm
she would have no choice
but to do his bidding
answer his calls
then he would be the alpha element

the Norwegians cobbled together little wooden boxes
nailed pieces of rotted driftwood
used many a white-out sheet
to protect the fairy people
but North Wind just kept blasting the air
blowing his trumpet
until he reached the entrance
to Elf's magic well

what North Wind didn't know
was although Enigmatic Elf was tiny and fragile
there lived a Force within her
one so strong
that no matter how much
he puffed his frozen snowfall
he would never defeat her powers
or own her abilities

for Elf had been given a very special gift
from the Universal Creator

That gift was love

to Elf's magic well

what North Wind didn't know was
although Enigmatic Elf was tiny and fragile
there lived a Force within her
one so strong
that no matter how much
he puffed his frozen snowfall
he would never defeat her powers
or own her abilities

for Elf had been given a very special gift
from the Universal Creator

That gift was love

Paul Girvan

We are the bees of the invisible

As a senior barrister and then as a judge Paul Girvan wrote extensively on legal matters during a long career. He now enjoys the freedom of creative writing particularly poetry, which is often inspired by his travels, by nature, by his sense of place, history and time and by his career in law. A keen amateur artist, his work is influenced by an artist's eye for colour, form and atmosphere. His prose piece Affairs of the Heart appeared in *Love, Loss and Cardiac Issues,* an anthology published by Impspired Press in 2022, and in 2023 his poetry was published in Issue 21 of the Impspired Online Magazine and the subsequent printed version. A contributor to North Coast Writers' 2023 Anthology *Spun Yarns and Woven Words,* his debut collection of poetry *In a Sense* was published by Impspired Press in 2024.

SKELLIG MICHAEL

A
grey
splinter
of bare rock
white foam footed
skyward steep ascends
Atlantic ocean's bastion spire
pointing to heaven's sombre silver
we land we mount on foot those steps
we climb that endless stairway open spiral
another Jacob's ladder angels now unseen
gargoyles that glint in sandstone and in slate
we cross Christ's slight green saddle and touch
heathered stones where sea pinks cling and smile
no busy bees buzzing now to fill those hill-top hives
gone bees of the invisible the monks who gathered nectar
made honey in stone desert gardens for their thirsty souls
and all the while great gangling gannets, gulls and guillemots
circling spin and plaintive sad they cry reel wheel and whine
if still guides the sailor's way the lighthouse on that rock
gather we still and taste true honey our storm tossed souls?
xxxxxxxxxxxxxxxxxxxxxxxxxxxxxxxxxxxxxxxxxxxxxxxxxxxxxxxxxxxxxxxxxxxxxxxxxxxxxxxxxxxxxxxxxxxxx
xxxxxxxxxxxxxxxxxxxxxxxxxxxxxxxxxxxxxxxxxxxxxxxxxxxxxxxxxxxxxxxxxxxxxxxxxxxxxxxxxxxxxxxxxxxxx
xxxxxxxxxxxxxxxxxxxx.   xxxxxxxxxxxxxxxxxxxx.   xxxxxxxxxxxxxxxxxxxxxxxxxxxxxxxx. .

Trouble up't Mill

Boulevard de Clichy Paris Moulin Rouge red mill
hirsute and stylish boulevardiers with time to kill
they come to sup a while and feast their wondering eyes
on sequined tights those ruffled skirts and thighs.

See nubile girls on swings above their tables high
all lightly clad and angel like they seem to fly
they tap to the tunes their feet in shoes of crocodile
and add to the place a louche and creepy style.

Cloaque de tous les vices sans the usual awful smell
that lingers round a place like this if truth we tell.

Perhaps we need to find a cleaner fresher place
a land of pure undriven snow and virgin space
no fleshpots there but only simple rustic stews
no boites de nuit ennui alluring girls or booze.

No canapés or champagne flutes so full of cheer
just simple wholesome pies and English ale and beer
though some might think that place just dull and dead
and long for another night in Place Pigalle instead.

The tentative subjunctive

Would that subjunctive's soft subtle sound
were still in vogue and still be found
peppering our words with gentle insinuation
would that it had not gone on long vacation
kinder than indicative at times so clipped
would that still out British mouths it tripped
could we but find for it far better use
take from imperative its sounding harsh abuse
more clever than conditional words their ifs and buts
less certain than the future which tricks us into ruts
certainty of things to come impossible to see
could we but mother tongue's descent escape and flee.

Would that we could stop turning you to youse
the Anglo-Saxon goodly ye turned woolly ewes
why are we now on chairs just sadly glumly sat?
that sounds prosaic ill-mannered maybe even fat
could we not yet again on seats and chairs just sit
or use the present participles that justly fit?
whoever saw sat president or saw sat duck
let's rehabilitate old word stood or simply chuck
were you to change a standing stone to stood stone
that would jar   would be quite against the tone
would that standing by the door you'd forebear to say
you're stood   for that bad education should betray.

Would that no-one cut our words to shreds insist
we marshal acronyms in lines   please do desist
U V F   S F   P I R A   poor DHSS
initials severed hacked a mangled verbal mess
would that past tense's words were truly fun
and not excruciating words like seen and done
could we but grammar's tools reread relearn
and on our bendèd knees devout and hopeful yearn
that Kingdom of King's English come back return
would that we could the gloried lustre buff up reshine
refill our heads with words refined repolished fine
and hear again the flow of words well spoken clear
that ink-dripped from the pen of great Shakespeare.

A-mused B-mused

The cornfields of my mind bare cut by sickle
now gone my muse, in favours promiscuous and fickle.
No more she strokes my head or whispers in my ear
the poet's empty now bereft and uninspired, I fear.

No more she turns to waspish verse heard words of talk
or wrestles rhyming couplets that, yes, might shock.
Where treads that wraith-like spectre now, that lass?
Flown off to different shores on beating wings, alas.

Why flit she far away - inflation or the banking crash?
Dispelled by passing worries or sight of dwindling cash?
Or sadly washed away by endless summer rains
clutching her posies Ophelia-like down dripping drains?

Perhaps the ageing of the poet brings forth a kind of doom
the sense of verse and fun cut short by darkening gloom.
The ticking of the clock brings forward now his many years
with all their serried ranks of stalking age-filled fears.

Or else the absence of good triggers from mealtime talk
that once inspired those verses full of mirth and mock.
Methinks the poet needs on stubble field new seed
to bring again the flighty muse, entice and gently feed.

So, gently coax that missing muse - be yet so very kind
to cast abroad new seeds to fill the cornfields of my mind
and maybe soon we'll see again fresh bowers new
and cornfields lit by sun awash with corn flowers blue.

Sour grapes

It was yet another one of those grey soft days in the West - dark blue purple tinged hills, a darkening cloudy sky hanging over the smudged hilltops slipping downwards offering only a few passing flashes of white light on the horizon. Tom and Jackie contemplated the scene through the steamed-up car window and half smiled half sighed. Yet another sunless honeymoon day on the Wild Atlantic Way. They drove along, each wondering why they had chosen to spend the first days of their married life in a dismal Irish West Coast summer.

Suddenly their spirit lifted somewhat when they saw an unfolding minor drama ahead of them on the road. A few boxes of cakes and bread were falling out of the back of a battered baker's van. The driver, oblivious to the mishap, drove onwards towards the distant village. Tom slowed and they contemplated the scene which at least diverted them from the murky misty gloom of the heavens which were now beginning to weep a fine mizzle.

Tom stopped and leapt out shouting "Waste not, want not!" Into the back of the car he lifted a box of whipped cream buns topped with green grapes. Jackie, ever conscious and proud of her svelte elegance tut tutted. "We really don't need those you know" she mockingly ticked off Tom. "Anyway, we just had breakfast."

They drove on. They saw a figure hunched over a bicycle pedalling slowly up the hill. Tom slowed down and lifted out the box of the cakes. He held it through the window to the passing cyclist, a middle-aged woman in a flapping colourless anorak and wearing a nondescript headscarf over her head. "Fancy these?" asked Tom. Eileen, for that was the name of the cyclist, looked bamboozled. Without thinking she took the box, put it in the panier with her shopping, muttered a few words of thanks and cycled on. Tom and Jackie drove on turning down a road to the left ahead of them. Eileen threw her eyes to the darkening heavens and muttered to herself " Tourists! They're going to go round in a circle that way. I bet I'll see them again."

As she cycled onward the mizzle turned to a more persistent drizzle then to a light rain and eventually it turned into a downpour. Eileen was getting soaked and went over to the side of the road and hunkered down into a thick gorse hedge to try and get out of the rain. As she hunched deep into the gorse she could feel its sharp prickles and the wetness of the rain from which she could not entirely escape. Her mood blackened like the sky. Who, she thought, were those eejits? Why on earth did she need a box of cakes? Why did they think she needed them? Northerners, she said to herself, they probably still think we're peasants living in the famine. The more she mulled over what had happened the more annoyed she became, the more patronised and slighted she felt. Her mood became darker and darker as the prickles pricked into her neck and the rain dripped over her.

After a while a car appeared. Tom and Jackie were back. I knew it, thought Eileen, they've gone round in a circle. Tom saw the woman hunched in the hedge. He opened the car window and shouted out "Get in, we can give you a lift to the village. We couldn't fit the cycle bicycle in - maybe you can come back for that later?" Before thinking Eileen climbed into the back of the car grabbing her shopping including the box of cakes. As they drove up the road now all puddled and muddy Eileen sat glumly in the back staring into the back of Tom and Jackie's heads. Their attempt at conversation with the woman was met by monosyllabic grunts. Silence descended. Eileen's dark mood had not been assuaged by the offer of a lift. Why did they think she needed charity? What planet were they living on? Do-gooders coming down here to insult the locals. It was all reminiscent of the souperism of the past, she thought.

When they reached the village, Eileen indicated where she wanted to get out. As she climbed out, she placed the box of cakes in the middle of the back seat and said to Tom "I don't eat cream buns - eat them yourself. Sure, don't you both look as though we need a good feed." With that she was gone.

Tom turned to Jackie. "As I said waste not, want not." He lifted the box from the back seat, took a bun and offered one to Jackie who reluctantly took it. When they took a mouthful, their pleasure was short lived. As the sour cream and grapes cream hit their pallet Tom burst out laughing: "What would that woman have thought of us if she had eaten these buns!"

Yvonne Hamilton

Let Sleeping Dogs Lie

A retired primary school teacher living in the seaside town of Portstewart in Northern Ireland, Yvonne Hamilton has been a member of North Coast Writers for three years. She started to write when forced to retire from a small amateur orchestra as poor night vision had made it unsafe for her to travel to rehearsals. That gave her the time - her dogs gave inspiration. In 2023 her first book, Fetch, a book of short dog stories, was published by Impspired Press. Other work was published in the Anthologies, Love Loss and Cardiac Issues, 2022, and Spun Yarns and Woven Words, 2023, both published by Impspired Press. In 2022 Yvonne read her own work at a Portstewart Library, Northern Ireland as part of the Aging Gracefully Initiative. Selections from Spun Yarns and Woven Words and Fetch were performed at St Paul's Tuesday Club, in Articlave, Northern Ireland, in June 2023.

Welcome Home

Hello Beatrice. Come in, come in. Did you have a good holiday?

Oh yes indeed but it's nice to be home. Pity about the rain. We had such sunshine on the cruise - every place we visited. Monaco, Rome, Venice, Naples - sunshine all the way.

Then it was a success I take it.

Absolutely. One meets such a nice class of person, you know. No riffraff. We had a top London ENT surgeon and his wife at our table. His wife was a leading speech therapist. And we had a man who had worked for Donald Trump at our table too. He had just retired. His wife was a bit, well, a bit inferior to him, I thought. But it's hard to judge with Americans, isn't it? Now where's my little man?

I have him in the snug. Come on through. I think he likes to see the other birds in the garden so I have his cage by the window.

Well well well, how's Mummy's wee man? I've been such a bad Mummy, going away and leaving you behind. But Mummy has got a present for you at home if you were a good boy. Were you a good boy for Auntie Florence?

You would hardly have known he was there most of the time.

He does look well. Have you grown a teensy bit while mummy was away? Doesn't he look so sweet when he ruffles his feathers like that? You do. You do.

Here's the bag with the rest of his food and a couple of his toys.

Now I hope you are free to come for coffee tomorrow morning. I'm sure you are dying to hear all about the cruise and see all the photos. Would eleven suit? Oh, and I have a little gift for you - should have brought it with me. Still, it will keep till tomorrow. A tea towel from Naples with little budgies all over it. So cute. Then you can think of my wee man every time you are drying your dishes! Come along, let's go and see Daddy. Till tomorrow at eleven then. Bye, thanks for looking after him.

Yes! That went well. She didn't suspect a thing! Now just bury the body and shred the receipt.

Doing Well

I thought that if I ignored it, it would go away. It didn't.

So I phoned my dentist

"Is it an emergency?" the voice on the other end enquired.

I was tempted to say yes but the story of the boy and the wolf flashed into my mind. "No" I admitted and hastened to add "But it's the sort of pain which could turn into an emergency tomorrow if it's not treated as an emergency today. It's Friday". I refrained from adding " If this turns into a throbbing crunching pain tomorrow when every dentist in the country is out on the golf course or playing rugby or mountain-biking or just plain sitting at home in front of the TV, what do I do then?" I didn't think it would further my case. Let that hover in the air.

The voice at the other end sighed "Let me see".

I waited.

"Could you come in at 3 o'clock?".

So, at three o'clock I am sitting in the dentist's chair bibbed and ready.

"Now Christine, what seems to be the problem?" he asks.

I explain, though I do not admit that I have no pain at the minute. I know it could pounce any time.

"Well then" he says "Let's take a look. Open wide" as he tips me back and starts to poke and tap around inside my mouth. When he comes to the offending tooth I jump.

"Yeees. A bit tender" he says as he tips me up again.

I wait.

"Mmmm. We need an x-ray". I bite down on the card, the machine works; we have a picture of the tooth. Just like that.

"Mmmm yes, as I thought, there is a bit of infection" he says, pointing to the picture. "Can you see it here?"

"Yes " I agree, not because I can see anything that I would recognize as a bit of infection but because that is what he expects me to say. After all ,it doesn't matter whether I can see it or not.

"Now" he says "That tooth is very fragile. In fact, it is largely made up of filling and there is a small pocket of infection below it in the gum. We have two options here. Either we treat it with a course of antibiotics in the hope that it settles down or .... we take it out. As I said before the tooth is fragile and may break up when I am removing it but it will almost certainly have to come out at some time in the future"

I realize that he has stopped talking and is waiting. I nod my head. Say nothing.

"What do you think? What should we do?" he prompts.

I don't know what we should do. I don't know what he should do. I need to say something. I remember a way out. "If I was your moth.......I stop. He has my birth date. He knows how old I am. I start again. "If I was your granny....," I hesitate again. He looks as if he should be sitting his A levels. Does he even shave yet? Perhaps I should say great grandmother? I start again "If I was your........... granny what would you advise?"

He smiles. He probably hears this two or three times each day – each person thinking they have found an original way of backing him into making the decision so he waits.

"Take it out if you can do it now," I say quickly. "I don't like the injections. I hate needles. Last time I had the hee-bee-jeebies. It was awful." I am babbling as his eyebrows demand an explanation. I take a deep breath "I shook all over. Couldn't stop. Turned into a shaking sobbing wreck. It was awful. I hate needles."

"Oh we can manage that," he assures me. "We'll be careful with your injection" as he tips me back.
"Open wide. Just a little scratch." he assures me as the needle goes in. I push back the urge to laugh. They used to say 'Just a little prick'. They don't say that anymore.
There is the rattling of instruments and quiet conversation with the dental nurse as we wait for the injection to work.

"You're doing well. Open wide," as he tips me back to poke and tap around in my mouth. I feel nothing.

"Good." he says as he sets to work on the tooth.

I feel him pushing and pulling, pulling and pushing, pushing and pulling.
He stops, moves away. I hear the clunk of an instrument

dropping into a tray.

Wow that was quick! I think to myself. Wrong!

"Open wide. You're doing well," as he proceeds to repeat the pushing and pulling accompanied by the shlushing of suction. Suddenly there is pain - real pain. Each time he presses the tooth.

"Ugh Ugh Ith ore," and I wave my open hands in front of me so that he stops, bringing me upright.

"Pain?" he asks.

I nod "esh"

He disappears behind me for some more rattling of instruments and quiet conversation before he tips me back. Then..........

"Just another wee injection. You're doing well" as the needle plunges.

Oh how I hate needles

A short wait.

Some tooth tapping before the pain free pushing and pulling resumes. I hear clattering of instruments on metal dishes. Is the tooth out? I hear a crunching sound. Is the tooth breaking up? My legs start to shake. I must stop them. I concentrate on relaxing my legs. As my legs relax my whole body starts to shake. Huge gulping sobs that I can't stop.

They are both beside me now.
The nurse touches me gently "Just breathe. You're doing well. Have a little rinse. Just breathe"
The cup is held to my mouth so that I suck water in but it dribbles out from my frozen lips to trickle down the bib. I try again – blood and water into the bowl. The nurse mops me up.

I breathe. The shaking has stopped.

"ith ith owth?" I ask

"Nearly there. You're doing well. Nearly there. Keep breathing" as he tips me back for more pushing and pulling.
"Keep breathing."
Instruments rattling into dishes then…..
He's standing beside me

"It's out" he says
But he doesn't tip me upright.
It's out. It's out. I relax and give a stiff, lopsided, frozen smile.

IT'S ALL OVER

He's still standing beside me. "You're doing well. Now just a few little stitches," he says.

The Great Escape

I knew that I might have waited too long. I wanted to hear the punch line of the joke - not just because the joke was funny, which it was, but the storyteller, Gregory, sitting opposite me at the round table was drop dead gorgeous and appeared to be unattached. So, it was a frantic dash for the ladies. As I entered the light came on. Made it. I slid the lock before sitting down, must stop doing that. You'll cut it too fine one of these days, you silly woman, I muttered as I prepared to return to the party.

I pushed the bar to open the door. It didn't move. On the second attempt the knob came off in my hand. I lifted it up to make sure that it really was broken. It was. I bent to look at the metal bar which secured the door to determine that the knob, now in my hand, had detached from the door. I was trapped - locked in, a prisoner, stuck in the lavatory.

"Hello" I shouted.

That was a waste of time. There's no-one there, you silly woman.

The words had hardly left my mouth when I heard the main door open followed by clicking of several sets of heels crossing the marble floor. The owners of the heels, laughing and shouting, ignored the lavatory stalls to renew make-up and spray perfume while keeping up boisterous conversations.

"Hello"

It was drowned out by a burst of laughter.

"Hello. I'm locked in."

Just heels and laughter still reaching me until the main door sighed as it closed. I had another look at the knob. It was still in my hand with no connection to the lock. Still useless. I looked round the space. There was a window - small, reinforced glass, set in a frame that did not allow for opening. Useless! and not even particularly good at letting light in.

Wait now. Wait now. The walls dividing the cubicles did not stretch as far as the ceiling. In fact ,there was quite a space above. Could I climb over the top of the partition?

I stood back to measure it with my eyes.

- stand on the toilet seat, mmm

- grab the top of the partition mmmm

- use the toilet roll holder for balance yes

- swing my leg up to hoist myself on to the top and drop down over the other side yes yes yes.

The great escape, you clever woman … but not in these shoes.

I removed the high heels, threw them over - I'd need them on the other side - to hear one clunk as it landed on the marble floor and the other......splash.

Before I had time to panic the main door opened

"Hello there. I'm stuck in here" as a pair of high heels tottered across the floor.

"Where are you?" said High Heels as they staggered along the line of doors thumping them one after the other muttering "Not here. Not here. Not here" as the doors clattered in turn back against the partitions.

When the last door failed to yield to two mighty thumps, the heels burst into song "I'm a jolly good fellow. Found you. You can come out now" followed by a bout of hiccoughs. "Door isn't open. Unlock your door. It's locked. The door's locked. Slide the wee bolt thingummy." Thump thump.

The heels tip-tapped into the cubicle next to me.

" Someone's put a shoe in the toilet bowl. I'd better not use this one. Did you hear that? Someone's put a shoe in the lavatory" Tap tapping into the next cubicle.

Heels clicked back to stand right outside my locked cubicle. Right up against the door so that I could see the points of the shoes in the space under the door. Thump Thump

"Do I know you? I'm Lily from Reception. What's your name?" More hiccoughs.

I knew Lily from reception. Everyone knew Lily from Reception - known in my department as The Town Crier - and I could imagine what she would make of the story should she be party to my rescue. I'd rather spend the rest of the night in the lavatory. So, I kept quiet.

I could hear her muttering against the door till she came to the conclusion that there might be a body behind the locked door then..........

"Must go and get help. Must get help. Don't go away now. Back in a minute. Don't go away."

The main door shut softly behind the retreating heels..

Time for action. Off with my skirt to be draped over the partition - couldn't throw it to risk it suffering the same fate as the shoe. I stepped up on the toilet seat, grabbed the top of the partition, balanced a foot on the toilet roll holder and swung my leg up to hook my foot on the top of the partition. I missed it and slithered back on to the toilet seat. It would need a stronger kick. Second time I hooked my foot over the top, pulled to secure my knee over the top, finally managing to drag my whole body along the top of the partition before tipping sideways to slide down on the other side.

Out. You clever woman! Now on with the skirt , on with the shoes, back to the party.

I pulled my shoe out of the toilet to wrap it in a huge bundle of toilet paper in the hope that by the time my skirt was on it might not actually have water running out of it. Now the skirt. There was no skirt. No skirt. It had fallen back as I scrambled over. It was locked in the cubicle I had just vacated. Here I was free as a bird in my sparkly top, my one dry shoe and a thong.

Why why why had I allowed myself to be coaxed into trying a thong. I'm not a thong sort of person. Thongs are all right for girls like Veronica – she is a dizzy sort of thong wearing type. I'm a sensible sort of knickers girl.

If someone comes here now what will you do, you foolish woman?

I heard the door open. Someone stepped into the room. My heart sank. What will I do? What will I do? I held my breath listening for more footsteps. Then a voice "Louise, Louise, are you in there? Are you all right?" a man's voice. I shivered. Couldn't speak.

"Louise, are you in there? It's Greg. Just let me know if you're OK. Lily has been wandering round claiming that there was a body and a shoe in the ladies' loo, and you had been gone for so long I thought I should check. Are you OK, do you need any help?"

I certainly needed help, but did I need it from Greg? If I refused, Lily might return or no-one else might appear. The function must be almost over, no-one else might come, I might be left here for the night.

I heard Greg move further into the room till he was standing outside the locked door. "Louise, just speak to me. I need to know that you're OK."

"My skirt is locked in the lavatory. I was locked in, but I climbed out. My skirt got left behind and my shoe fell into the lavatory." I could feel that the tears were not far off. If he laughs now - if he laughs now…

"Let me get this straight. You are alive and well and standing skirtless in this cubicle," tapping the door behind which I was shaking. "Your skirt is locked in this next cubicle," tapping the locked door of that one. " Have I got it right?"

"Yes. Could you look under the door? maybe you could see it to pull it out."

I heard him scuffle down. "No. it's too far in." Back on to his feet. "I have an idea. It will take me a minute or two to find what I need but I'll be straight back."

I sat on the toilet seat resigned to a wait. He was back in no time.

"Here, wrap this round yourself and come out. I'll need your help to reach your skirt" passing a hotel towel through the doorway.

With the towel wrapped securely round me - all trace of a thong hidden - I emerged from the cubicle to see Greg leaning against a basin swinging a golf club. Yes swinging a golf club - a putter. Before I could do more than open my mouth he wagged his finger "Now listen before you start. We're both going to lie face down, I'll use the club to snag the skirt and when I get it near enough you grab it. OK?

I did as I was told. I could see my skirt. It was less than a club-length away. Greg pushed the club in to hook it under the skirt. It slipped off so he tried again managing to snag it and bring it within my reach.

I heard the door open, a trembling voice said "Oh no! Oh no! " before the door closed on a departing woman.

"Get this skirt on quickly till we get out of here before someone else arrives - I don't fancy trying to explain all this. Can you imagine what they would make out of Poor Louise who was Locked in the Lavatory?"

He opened the door pulled me out along the corridor to the main reception which was abuzz with people too busy talking to notice us. "Straight for the door now, don't stop to speak to anyone. I have to visit the Gents. Meet me at the main door. Then it's straight to my car. I'll drive you home."

As the car doors clunked shut I was amazed, shocked to hear him snort with laughter. If he starts to sing "Oh Dear What Can The Matter Be" …

He burst out into a shout of laughter almost choking. I turned round to confront him to find him pressing his fingers to my lips.

"No shush, Louise listen . Listen to me. They are all panicking in there about two bodies which have been discovered in the ladies' loo. Someone told the manager that there were two dead bodies lying in the ladies' loo. They are talking about calling the police. We need to get out of here. I'm sure you don't want to have to explain that, do you?"

As we left the car park I felt his shoulders shaking, I felt the laughter start to bubble up in me so that by the time we had reached the town it could not be contained. He pulled the car over. We laughed till we cried. I had never understood that saying before, but we did. we laughed till we cried.

That was over thirty years ago. We laugh about it still.

Conundrum

In this part of the world we have people who know people, people who know people who know people, people who think they know people. The rest just get on with minding their own business. I belong in the last category.

My name is David Brown. I am a country wide sales representative for a large company selling paint and wallpaper. Though I am a firm believer in the principle of mind your own business I was, at one time, embroiled, very reluctantly, in the dealings of the other groups. This is how it came about.

Since the local sales rep for knitting wool was dragged out and beaten up after wandering into the wrong pub with a red white and blue check scarf dangling from his coat pocket I exercise a measure of care over where I go for business. They didn't kill him but the wheel chair served as a grim warning to all sale reps. ever after. So there are places where I would not go should I never sell a tin of paint or roll of wallpaper again: places where I enter with care, always mindful in my choice of colours; my shirt, my coat, my scarf, even my tie. It might be the difference between life and death.

On the day in question I had an appointment with John, a customer in a fringe area of the city where a couple of streets away it merged into a no go region for police and army. I parked on the street facing up the hill on which his shop stood, locked my car and, with my brief case under my arm, made my way across the road, down the couple of hundred yards to the shop. The sun was shining but the street was not crowded. Two cars passed me on their way up the hill, a woman pushed a buggy down the opposite footpath, two little girls were skipping near the bottom of the hill, three older women chatted further up. All normal. Still, in a street on the fringe it pays to be careful.

I met John at the door of the shop to make our way to the café next door where we usually did business. Over a leisurely lunch we finalised an order, exchanged family news before making arrangements to meet up for a game of golf at the start of the next month. Afterwards, while I waited to cross the road I noticed that the two girls were drawing chalk pictures on the pavement now. The three older women were replaced by two younger women with buggies. I checked my watch pleased to see that, with the order placed by John, my quota for the rest of the week was met. I should manage a few holes of golf before dinner with a bit of luck. Two cars went by before I nipped across the road. I unlocked the car, opened the door, flopped on to the warm seat with my briefcase on my knee, inserted the key.

As I was about to start the engine the door was wrenched open. I turned to grab the door, prepared to deal firmly with the person who stood there.

I found myself staring at a gun.

A swift glance up,that revealed two cold gray eyes staring out from a masked face, convinced me that this was no child with a toy gun. This was a man who meant business. My insides seemed to melt while my heart raced in my throat.

"Get out!"

This couldn't be happening. It was broad day light. There were people on the hill, cars passing, it couldn't be happening.

"Get out " he growled, waving the gun.

"Get the fuck out." pointing the gun at my head.

I stumbled out still clutching my briefcase.

He jumped in, started the car and roared off up the hill out of sight.

I staggered backwards on weak legs that threatened to collapse completely beneath me till I grabbed a window sill where I managed to prop myself. I looked round. No-one was looking at me. No-one seemed to have noticed. No-one was coming to help me. I sat on the window sill, clutching my briefcase, bent over to allow the lambeg drumming of my heart to subside, fighting for breath.

"You alright, mister?"

He looked about twelve years old. Too young to be a threat, perhaps. But he made me realize that I should move.

"Yes. Yes thanks. OK I I I'm OK" I muttered over my shoulder as I lurched away towards John's shop. Where else could I go!

John ushered me into his office. It took several minutes for the whiskey to start its work. Several more for me to manage to explain.

"Well, at least they didn't take your briefcase. Something to be thankful for."

I looked round. I couldn't see it. "Where ?"

"It's under my desk. Relax. You came in clutching it as if your life depended on it. I managed to coax you to swap it for a whiskey."

We sat in silence till I began to see beyond the disappeared car and the gun.

"I suppose I need to contact the police. OK if I use your phone? Or do I need to go to the police station? What do you think?"

"We…..ell, Dave old man…………………..I'm not sure that they can do very much. I mean your car is certainly inside the no-go area by now."

"You think I shouldn't go to the police?"

"We…..ell…………………..did you recognize the gun man, would you know him if you saw him again? What was it you said he was wearing jeans, a black top and a mask – that could be any young blade in the town. The police can't go far on that, can they!"

I shook my head remaining silent.
John put his hand on my shoulder

"Now......................I might be able to do something. I'm not promising anything but I might be able to contact someone. Not promising anything now. Want me to put out a few feelers?"

I nodded.

"But if we can't get the car back I'll need a police report for insurance. It's a company car. They'll need a police report before the insurance will pay out"

John scratched his head.

"Tell you what" as he reached me a set of keys "Take my car now to get you home. Come back tomorrow afternoon. That gives me time to see what I can do. If it doesn't work out you can still go to the police. How does that sound?"

I nodded.

One hour and two cups of coffee later John was waving me off from his house with his reassuring message ringing in my ears "See you tomorrow. Don't worry. They only want the car, they don't know anything about you. If they had your briefcase it might be different but they haven't got it. They are not interested in you, they don't know where you live, you're OK don't worry They don't know you and you don't know them."

It was a relief to leave the lights of the city behind. Driving conditions were good: a light wind; clear skies with a full moon; very little traffic. Even driving slowly it would not take too long to reach home. I turned on the radio to find soothing relaxing music.

Then It hit me like a punch to the stomach so that I veered, nearly hitting the ditch. As I swerved towards the side of the road I heard the angry blast of the horn from the car behind me before it pulled out to overtake. I drove slowly, carefully to the lay-by. Pulled in.

How could I have forgotten?
How could I have forgotten?
My golf clubs. My new golf clubs. My new very expensive golf clubs. My new very expensive golf clubs that Alison knew nothing about. The ones I had bought after convincing her that we could not afford the tumble drier that she really really needed. She couldn't seem to understand the importance of the golfing fraternity in my business, of how many of my orders were finalised on the golf course. I had given up trying to explain.

Those new golf clubs were in the boot of the car.

I sat with my hands on the steering wheel, my head on my hands as a plan took shape. **Alison must not find out**. The money for the driver alone would possibly have bought one or two tumble driers. I looked at my watch. With any luck she would be asleep by the time I arrived home. I'd leave John's car at the golf club car park, cross the road home, so she need never see the strange car. She would not question an empty drive way – I frequently walked home from the club - but a strange car would require an explanation. And I could see where that would end.

It all worked beautifully so I woke next morning feeling quite positive in time to phone John to ask for his help with the recovery of my clubs. Done while Alison was in the shower – she need never know, she need never worry.

I bought a bottle of his favourite whiskey to give to John by way of a thank you. After lunch I set off for the city convinced that I would be driving home later in my own car – with my precious clubs in the boot. I parked on the same side of the street as I had done the previous day but a little further up the hill. As I locked the car a small girl of about seven or eight - the same age as my Lucy - ran up to shove an envelope into my hand.

"I was told to give you this, Mr Brown" she called out before racing off up the hill to disappear round the corner at the top. I didn't know her, had never seen her before. I had no idea where she came from nor where she went. Though I could see the usual number of people on the street she did not seem to belong to any of them. No-one was looking for her. No-one was looking at me. I had the eerie feeling that they all knew about me yet I was invisible. I squeezed the envelope. A bulky letter? – stuffed it in my pocket, hurried across the road.

John met me at the door.

"Someone will be coming about the car, David. After closing time. I got word through about your clubs too so it looks good"

I pulled the envelope out of my pocket. I waved it in front of him muttering "Look at this! What on earth is this? A little girl no older than my Lucy handed it to me just one minute ago. For Mr Brown she said. She knew me, she knew my name"

John took the envelope "Let's see" He slit it open, tipped it up, dropping the contents into the palm of his hand. We both stared in disbelief. I was first to speak
"Alison's family allowance book"

We stared at it in silence then I burst out "How did they get this? They've got Alison . They must have broken into my house. Maybe taken the children. I must go. How can this be happening?"

As I turned to rush out John put out a restraining hand on my arm "No no no no no Wait a minute. Wait a minute. Let's give this a bit of thought. Don't be rushing into anything." I allowed myself to be drawn up to his office. "Now listen to me David. That's not the way they work. Would the book have been in your car by any chance? Could it have been in your car, Dave?"

I shook my head "I don't think so. Alison usually keeps it in her bag. I don't think so."

"Take your time. Did you take her to collect her family allowance last month? Did she borrow your car to collect it herself, maybe? When was the last time you saw the book?

Of course. I remembered. After collecting the money, she had left the book in the glove compartment before we went shopping for a new kitchen table a couple of weeks ago.

"There you are. That's how they knew your name, That's how they knew you. They have your car, they're not interested in you, you don't know them – you're no threat. Now let's go next door for something to eat. With a bit of luck you might be driving home in your own car before bedtime."

The light was fading before we heard the rattle at the locked shop door which John opened to admit a plump little grey haired lady dressed in a navy jacket and skirt. She had a homely look – she reminded me of my granny. She bustled in to shake hands. "I'm Mary" as she put her fingers to her lips and shook her head "No names please. It's better that way. I believe you are looking for an item that has gone astray. You can look on me as your fairy god-mother. I think I can restore your property to you. I don't wave a magic wand but I've come to take you to collect it"

My question of "Am I getting my car back?" elicited a shake of her head.
"Well not today, son. It does sometimes happen. It depends on what the job happens to be. Sometimes there is no car to give back, you understand. Depends on the job. But golf

clubs are a different matter. I'm to take you to collect them." she twinkled.

"You didn't bring them?"

"No no that's not the way it works, son. You have to come and collect them. I'll take you, OK?"

I hesitated. I felt safe here in the shop with John. Mary was waiting, smiling at me. John nodded his head "That's good news isn't it? and if you come back here afterwards I'll drive you and your clubs home whatever time it is"

I found myself nodding also. This was no man in a mask brandishing a gun. This was Mary standing smiling at John in John's shop. What harm could come to me with this wee old woman.

I sat beside her in silence as she drove. We meandered through parts of the city that were unknown to me till at last she pulled the car into a lay-by beside what looked to be a park. I could see a row of terrace houses at the top of a slight slope on the other side of the road.
"Now this is as far as I go" as the engine was switched off "You need to get into the back seat, son and someone will be with you shortly"
She must have seen the horror on my face "Sorry, you thought that I would be bringing you to the clubs. It doesn't work like that. It takes one of them to do the business with those boys. You'll be OK, son. Just hop into the back".
By the time I had clambered into the back seat she had disappeared.

It was dark, the lights on the row of terrace houses did not filter down as far as the lay-by, there were no lights in the park. I was terrified, my teeth chattered, my insides churned. I should get out and run for it I thought for one foolish second. But I had no idea where I was or where I could run to. The smell of cigarettes lingered in the car. It triggered a powerful desire for a smoke. I hadn't smoked for years. I rubbed my hands together to warm them before sticking them up my sleeves. I cursed the clubs. I should just have walked away, minded my own business, got on with my life.

The door of the car was thrown open.
I scrambled across towards the other door as the clubs clattered in and the door slammed.
I sat up straight to peer around.
It was quite dark. I could see nothing .
I held my breath.

The driver's door opened. Someone climbed in.
Someone tall. Someone smelling of cigarettes.

Silence.
The engine started.
The car moved, bumped out of the lay-by gathering speed quickly. I sat hunched up against the door behind the driver so I couldn't see his eyes in the rear-view mirror. I didn't want to see him. I did not want him watching me.

Soon we were travelling through deserted streets, deserted streets brightly lit

We were back in a part of the city which I knew well, not far from John's shop, before the car stopped.

"Get out. Take your clubs and get out"

I opened the door with shaking hands dragging the clubs after me.

As I slammed the door he lowered his window so that a pair of cold grey eyes looked me straight in the eye.

"Did you get your wife's family allowance book back?" before he drove off

He might as well have said

Remember, we know where to find you if we ever need to.

That was all of three years ago. Since that Alison has become the proud possessor of a tumble drier though she discovered almost immediately that she really really needed a new sofa What has it done to me you may well ask? Well, I like to think that I am still a man who just gets on with minding his own business. I do wonder if I am now a man who knows a man who knows a man or if I am a man who **thinks** he knows a man.

I try not to wonder about John.

Brenda McAteer

Retired and living in Portrush, a seaside town in N Ireland, Brenda joined North Coast Writers in 2020. With their help and support stories that used to wander round her head are now appearing on paper. A flash fiction piece No Walk No Escape was performed at Orchard Flash Festival 2021 and can be found on YouTube at www.byddielee.com/flash-fiction-armagh. In 2023 another Flash Fiction piece Reflections was performed at the Armagh Museum 2023 event, available at the same YouTube link. In 2022, a memoir piece, Watch Cup was published by Northworld NI, and two further pieces in 100 Voices – NI, 100 Years, BCRC. Her work can also be found in three anthologies Irish Hares and Seahorses, Love, Loss and Cardiac Issues, and Spun Yarns and Woven Words published by Impspired Press in 2022 and 2023.

Immersion poem

lie back breathe
burrow into the blanket
view   gaze   embrace
as iconic images
flood the senses

vacant church
reimagined for images
colours   shades   shapes
swirl round walls and floors
feelings heighten

starry night
floods the animated space
vibrant   awesome
daubs of yellow encircled stars
shadowy cypress

gratitude
shown through sunflowers
thirty   shades   of yellow
painstakingly captured
full bloom to droop

shed blanket
glide to don VR headset
absorbed   engaged
within his studio then bar
dizzy with delight

exposed bared
Van Gogh genius uncovered
visionary   psychotic
frenetic toil fantastic art
sold one painting

Tat Off!

One year ago, Shay and I ran out of our last A level, picked up our rucksacks and headed to the airport. Off to Magaluf to join Jamie and the others. They'd been there two days and the photos were class. Jamie promised to meet us at the airport.

Twenty WhatsApps later, a very pale Jamie met us from the bus.

'Got the sun then,' we snorted.

Jamie just said follow me. We arrived at a dodgy looking apartment block, crawled up six floors into a cramped alcohol and piss smelling space with cushions and bodies everywhere. Jamie told us it's booked for four but we're eight now.

'If the door goes four of us have to get out on the balcony and climb next door. They do the same if their door's knocked'.

We cracked open the first bottle and cheered, let the party begin! Oh yes, it began and went on non-stop for four days. The day started at 6pm, all emerging and fighting for the bog and the shower. Attempts to look cool in the white shorts that weren't white after night one.

The lads had a plan.

6pm Pub crawl round the centre with a must have burger to soak up the alcohol, they were religious about that.

10pm chat up the girls who were equally drunk so they would agree to anything - well - we hoped so.

Midnight and the rush to the Clubs. Vast neon spaces, flashing lights, music, mad DJ's, half naked dancers, shots, tabs and girls.

Rave to 6am, chippie on the way back, sleep, throw up and start again at 6pm. Fanfuckingtastic.

As we staggered back on the last night Shay spotted a tattoo parlour.

'We're eighteen now let's get a tattoo' he slurred.

I don't really remember the next hour, vague jabs of pain and separated from my last 50 euro.

Next morning hangover from hell, aching knuckles.

' Shay, were we in a punch -up?'.

'No, tattoos, Jack the lad'.

'Where, what did I get?'

'The tattooist was getting narked so when he said what's your favourite food, girl or word, you shouted fuck'.

I tried to focus and there it was on each hand, all glorious curls and colour. I just retched.

Back home, Ma went for me with a rolling pin,

'You might be eighteen but you're a pathetic drunken dope!'

She was right, I had an interview for the police service coming up. Six hundred applications and I'd got into the last sixty. Not the best message to give as you shake hands with the interview board.

A week later we went to a local tattooist who smirked,

'Been in Magaluf then?

It's as well you're called Jack,'

'You can thank me later', roared Ma.

He re-imaged one Fuck to Jack, the other became Luck.

I got through the interview, loving the training and slowly but surely spending my allowance having my pictorial memory of Magaluff lasered off!

Starry Night

At last, sitting outside the café portrayed in Van Gogh's masterpiece set in Arles. I've had a poster of the painting on my wall for years. Just to be here to feel to gaze to relax.

When I spotted the ad for an art and meditation course in the Arles region, I booked without a thought. In between jobs, relationships and the wrong side of thirty, this will be the boost I need.

I imagined sitting under those stars, wine in hand, breathing in Van Gogh's genius, streaming Starry, Starry Night through my I phone. Don McLean, another of my creative icons. It would be bliss. The creative forces that drove Van Gogh and McClean would inspire me and my next painting would stun and shine.

Course complete we all head to the café. Reclining on a chair outside it, breathing in the warm French air, glass of local white wine in hand, with a group of perfectly lovely people. Why do I feel disenchanted?

There are no stars tonight. It's been overcast and cloudy since we arrived. The café is still a beautiful yellow ochre, but the sky is not a glorious deep blue.

Heading through Dublin airport, I had grabbed a magazine. McClean's name on the cover. Serendipity I thought. The article stunned me. It was written by his ex-wife. After decades of controlling manipulation, she left, and now runs support groups for other trapped women. Painful when heroes crash to the floor.

Our effete tutor was agog at Van Gogh and his art but also - as he sees it - his magnificent descent into madness. This, Jean-Luc pronounces led to hundreds of wonderful paintings. I now see an artist struggling with mental health issues and low self-esteem. Another icon becomes human.

Today I presented my three-day odyssey of an oil painting - depicting my current angst. Harsh, dull metallic stars with deep blue tears raining down on dying sunflowers. Jean Luc ran over and clutched me to his bony body – an uncomfortable moment. He took me by the hand to a double meditation class. I cried, sobbed and was perhaps reborn as the others walked around me keening. So glad no one else from Ireland is on the course.

Nonetheless, sipping my wine I do feel this weird week has taught me something. As I sit outside the marvellous street café, with sympathetic nods from my fellow failed artists, I feel released. I vow in future I'll search for my own stars, my own images, my own words - not those of others, especially not my icons,

'Garcon, un autre vin blanc, s'il vouz plait'.

My Street

Jackie stomped down the street. His street. Face burning roast red, choking, shaking with resentment. Muttering, 'You fool, you're a laughing-stock, a chump, a mug'.

He usually sauntered with his head held high, arms swinging, nodding to all and sundry, reminiscing. On this street he'd been

pushed in a pram
toddled around
played 5-a-side and hand ball
swung off the lampposts
played knock and run
run amok with the lads
smoked, downed cider
and dated girls in the back alley.

His street.

Today his head was imploding. He fumed, This street, my street, my centre, they can't do this to me. He banged in his front door, slamming it shut, then physically deflated as he slumped against the wall.

He'd mooched up and down this street for the last twenty-eight years, his parents for thirty or so before that, and at least one set of grandparents back to the turn of the last century, when this dockland red brick terraced street was built. Their street, his street and in his scheme of things his kids' street. Until now, he sighed, as he sank to the floor.

Jackie had felt constant, fixed even, as the street changed over the last couple of decades. As neighbours moved out, his P4 class got smaller.

His mother lamented, 'There's the Platts and McGiverns gone, joining that crowd heading out of the city to the hills, and those big blank estates.'

With growing sons now shaving and the daughters perming and colouring in her kitchen sink, she could see the advantages of an inside bathroom. But those new estates were miles from the city centre and the shops.

Patting Jackie's head, her youngest, 'Not for the likes of us, we're city folk'.

More families left. For a while, houses lay empty. The area began to look run down.

The Primary School numbers shrank from 250 to 100 kids by the time he was heading to the big school. Then the real changes started. Families from faraway places moved in. Kids of all colours and languages arrived on the street and in his classroom. Strange clothes, even stranger religions. His mother warned him to be polite - 'just don't ask them round'. He hadn't planned to.

Everyone stuck to their own. Jackie with Jimbo and Digger - the real local lads. But then before they knew it, Farouk (Rookie) and Mohammed (Mohawk) had joined them at the youth club and turned out to be great craic. The street had changed but settled again.

Jackie, like his Dad, left school at sixteen to train as a plumber. Rookie and Mohawk went on to do A Levels. They didn't move back to the street, but Jackie kept an eye on their parents, helping out if needed. All his brothers and sisters had moved too, most to the city outskirts or further for work. He stayed … to look after his parents, but more because he couldn't see himself anywhere else.

~ ~ ~ ~ ~

Last night, wee Maisie had a temperature and an angry rash. Anita phoned 'Out of Hours'. They agreed to send a Doctor. When Jackie opened the door an hour later he roared,

'Holy crap, Mohawk, what are you doing here?'

'Doctor Mohawk to you, Jackie lad', laughed Mo.

Once they had sorted out Maisie had an ear infection, no danger of meningitis, they yarned, remembering good and not so good times on their street. Mo had bought a house in the suburbs, and joked about his middle-class life and 2.4 kids.

'Imagine! Me! The son of Pakistani runaways.'

Mo asked Jackie why he was still here, now he had his own family and a plumbing business.

'It's my street Mo, can't see myself anywhere else. Anita would like a garden, a better school for the kids but everything's on the doorstep here. I know every kerbstone. My roots are here.'

'Jackie, you'd fit in anywhere. You've a way of making people feel safe, you could do that anywhere. I still tell people about you and the lads calling Rookie and me the black and tan! And in the Youth Club you were the one who stopped others picking on us.'

'Awh, don't make me cringe Mo'.

'Jackie, think of your kids' future. Give them more space if you can? The area's getting run down. Rentals go to social cases now. My parents are going to move in with us. Pa said the only thing he'll miss here is you. He says you're old school - all about family, hard work and community.'

Jackie promised to take the family to visit Mo but felt uneasy. 'All very well for Dr Mo to move and fit into a snob's area, that's not really for me.'

~ ~ ~ ~ ~

Their conversation spurred Jackie to go to the local Housing Office. He'd been avoiding this. He hadn't told the Housing Association he was the main householder now. His father passed away three years ago. His Mum stayed with Anita and him until her dementia meant a move to a Care Home nearly a year ago.

The wee clip of a girl behind the desk laughed in his face when he explained why he was there, calling in the Supervisor.

'No, Mr McCurdy the house won't automatically go to you. Passing from one generation to the next only happened when these houses were owned by private landlords. It's a Housing Association now. In fact, now your father's passed away and your mother's moved to a Home, you have no right to the property. We'll set up a time limited agreement to give you the opportunity to find new accommodation – six months maximum. We house families in need Mr McCurdy. You can go on the list, but you'll need points to prove your eligibility.'

Jackie was handed a pile of forms.

~ ~ ~ ~ ~

He sat on his hall floor, head in his hands, stunned.
Vulnerable, scared, shaken,
My safe place - gone.

Maisie ran to Jackie. 'Daddy sad, hug Daddy', as she climbed on top of him.

'Awh, wee Maisie, amn't I the fool thinking Georgie or you would take on this house in years to come. Mo's right, the world's changed, the street's changed. I'm a fool, Maisie, a sentimental eejit.'

Picking Maisie up he called to Anita,

'Wait til you hear the cheer Maisie, when I tell your Ma we have to move. Our ears will be ringing'.

He stood up, breathed in, put on his 'Jackie in charge' face.

'Here's to a garden for your Ma, with a swing and climbing frame for you and Georgie. Our future, on a new

street
road
avenue
close
… whatever.'

Orla McFaul

Living in Bellaghy, a village in the North of Ireland with her family, after taking various writing courses, Orla Mc Faul joined North Coast Writers in 2021. She performed two of her poems '*Twilight*' and '*Changing Focus*' at the Seamus Heaney Homeplace in 2021. Her poems can be found in *Autumn Fragments*, a pamphlet edited by Jessica Traynor in 2021, and in three anthologies, *Irish Hares and Seahorses* and *Love, Loss and Cardiac Issues*, and *Spun Yarns and Woven Words*, all three anthologies published by Impspired Press.

Steadfast Sun Misty Moon

In the early morning light
I sit with my heart
battered   bruised

but hopeful still
hopeful as dawn

a tentative sun peeps over the horizon
wonders what the day will bring
what the world will show

a warming sun
holds firm
weathering storm after storm

not always seen   but always there
unhurried   until dusk
then trusting the moon to take watch

two halves   one heart
in the sky
parental   custodians of our world

steadfast sun   misty moon
ruling time   tide   life
beating   clockwork

heart balm
healing for the soul
when all around is fleeting

If I had wings   I'd go too

It's the dying
the beginning of the end
running out of time

It's the jobs undone
the dreams unhad
unfulfilled

It's the closing in
closing up
sudden chill in a breeze

true there is a beauty in the changing colours
of the changing season
a peace in nature's acceptance
everything is as it has to be

autumn bleeds into unforgiving winter
in a turn of the sky
in the blink of an eye

even the birds leave
they too
do not like autumn

The Soul Before

you called to me
for years   yearning

haunting from before-life
until I could no longer deny you

I saw you in my dreams
asleep and awake

when I met you
your cry   a familiar song

a memory from somewhere
someone my soul already knew

your delicate beauty
unfamiliar   recognised

in this life
like a slow sigh

sitting after years of standing
a weight lifted
a new one bestowed

fracture

it could have been a disaster
later I shudder   thinking
what ifs   maybes

an everyday task
saddle and bridle on
standing close

my hands on you soothing
I feel your wild heart
beating

then you are rearing
spooked by sudden distant
banging

I grab your reins
pull you down
to save her

falling
my left foot takes your weight
mirrors my swollen belly

nothing ever the same
our connection changed
with my new life

despite the pain   I am grateful
when I look back   at the days end

I would do it all again

Balm

we buried her
turned home

in the emptiness where life was lived
we gather together for comfort?
or perhaps we don't know anything else

fracture lines are there
fissures deeper menacing
without the balm

unravelling begun long since
faster now bufferless

all calm is in the ground
in the dark rotting earth
powerless at the vengeance

all turning

the murmur of a miracle

Jimmy Milliken

Having grown up in Northern Ireland Jimmy Milliken spent much of his adult life in the Shetland Islands, but currently lives near Ballycastle on the north coast of Ireland.

He has twice been shortlisted for the Seamus Heaney Poetry Award; in 2018 for his poem Mercy Killing and in 2020 for Lichen. His poem The Butt was longlisted for the 2019 Bangor Literary Journal Poetry Competition. Another poem Colloquy was shortlisted for the 2020 Bangor Literary Journal 40 Words Competition and appears on YouTube. He has performed his poetry at various showcase events and readings throughout Ireland, including at The Seamus Heaney Homeplace in Bellaghy, in Portstewart, Ballymoney, Ballycastle, Limavady and most notably on a mountain top in Connemara.

His first poetry collection, Cracking the Air, was published by Impspired in 2022. Further poems have featured in three anthologies published by Impspired, a chapbook Autumn Fragments published by Seamus Heaney Homeplace, and in every annual Community Arts Partnership Anthology published between 2016 and 2023. In October 2023 he won the inaugural Soundwaves Competition prize for Best Performance Piece for his poem *walking the strand.*

the circus is in town

blazing sun blaring horns big bass drum grass burnt brown
   lions' cage   poke & roar   cymbals crash   forest fire
  jugglers clowns elephants   frilly capes & dancing apes
ticker tape & date rapes   & elephants
         elephants on parade
                  elephants' last decade

jugglers clowns sword swallowers fire eaters eating
  fire   & twilit tents where freaks sleep
     & keep their secrets close
       care for a peak - you know you do
behind these folds of curtains where dark eyes shine
& mermaids dine & skeletons & blade in teeth
half man half beast is eating rats alive
               cyclops

   & clippiddy clop troupes of horses white
pink sequined lady pirouettes on stallion's back
        ring master cracks the whip
         matinee   evening show
            & late night thrills
             guaranteed

       the circus is in town

& desolation crow
slow spun   scratch on wire   scrape of rust
breeze gusts   and whips a demon   from the dust
a scattering of crows   hauled up from burnt red earth
black rags they flutter   in and out of being
shriek and freeze on skeletal trees
branches   withering

hammer heart in hollow chest   deep down   urges
thumps and thrusts   drives whining   wailing
black smoke thick   blots livid skies
tendons   trailing
screech of string stretched   raked and ripped
slashed & lacerated   stripped back shock
wide whites of eyes   saw bone serrated

from railroad tracks & crossroads
old back porch warbles
strung up on lamp posts
on main street

the circus is in town

elephants on parade

1.

round the ring & round & round
& round & round & round   & round
keep 'em steady   keep it smooth
trunk on tail on trunk on tail
on trunk
draped in pink

round the ring & round & round
& round & round & round   & round
draped in pink
cap & cape & uniform
they can't escape they must conform
they will perform
tail on trunk on tail on trunk
on tail
popcorn tinsel ginger ale
crack the whip swing the flail

don't spoil the beast   don't spare the rod
crack the whip   drive 'em hard
fire & fear & cattle prod
don't give a sod
for welfare

cattle prods & iron rods drive 'em hard don't give a sod
on they plod   on they plod
don't give a sod
for welfare
childcare
nightmare
lord's prayer

trunk to tail to trunk   to tail
  to trunk
            to
  round   & round

2.

round & round in their capes and caps while
when he cracks the whip
you can hear it all round the ring

& the pretty blonde woman in sequins
right in the middle   all graceful twirls
& he cracks it again   the band plays
climb upon my knee sonny boy
& they stop & sit on each other's knees
& we all laugh & go
aaawww

then the music stops   the drums roll
& the pretty blonde woman in sequins
lies down in the sawdust   head on a block

crack   *carrack* snaps the whip

& the really big one with the broken tusks
leaves the herd & trump trump trumps real loud
& puts his great foot on the pretty blonde woman's head

we all tremble   the drum rolls stop
we hold our breath   mummy squeezes my hand
till it hurts

then he cracks his whip
& the really big one lifts up his great foot
& not a bit of sawdust   no not one bit   has dropped in her hair
& the pretty blonde woman in sequins
jumps up & waves her arms in the air
graceful circles graceful circles
we cheer & cheer for ages & ages
& they trot round the ring once more

then out they go to get chained up in cages
till this time tomorrow
or maybe the next day
or maybe the one after that

lion tamer

I put my head in Simba's mouth
old abattoir breath steaming
saliva mucous drip & lick
drip
lick

Friday matinee

clouds of flies hung in the air
burnt sugar jumbo dung

the horns squeaked east
the drum roll pattered
away into the void

crowd held its breath
beast jaws & teeth
king of the jungle
all mange and lice
lump of rancid meat

clowns covered their eyes mock terror
Lil & Pink Sequined Sal
arm-in-arm shared a cheroot
& tongues

a woman high in the stalls released
the scream of a demoness
Simba stirred
I cracked the whip
the sawdust is there
to suck up tears & blood

Flying trapeze

caged bird razzle soars through dreams
   high in the vaulted big top   lights dimmed
& focused   intense beams ignite
   white limbs   & rainbow
                                    sparkle
                                               flash
                                                      sequins

the air electric   & all the little budgies gawk
   eyes uplifted   jaws slack
   popcorn & jellybeans forgot

                              the aerial ballet
          high above the net

waltzing through the air in pirouette
   half turns & passing leaps
 double   triple   quadruple somersaults
   she swoop   she fly   she free bird
  night sky shooting star   blaze in dark

       galaxy goddess   demon   angel
                 nova-
                          nova-
                                 supernova

& then suspended from the bar
clinging by teeth
she spins in spotlight
swirl & whirl & all is nothing
an incandescence in the void

hot night & sequin glitter
sweat & flies
& grease

& descends
with
a
thousand
hearts

sawdust beneath the net
decay disease

do elephants have fleas

after the late show

steamy night   sweat   dripping   moths & lamplight   long
gone midnight   this runaway kid
shows   trembling

I'm with the gang drinking cheap ruby wine   in the
powdered dirt 'side of Pugsie's 'van
locked in a circle of truth or dare   heard the half of it before
not that that matters a
damn

Myrtle in the middle halfway through her disappearing beer
bottle trick   & the kid
squeaks   *oh where'd that bottle go*
& Myrtle grins her missing teeth   *come on over and get a taste*
of it kid   then you'll
know

over by the cages shooting craps   Pascal & Doogie & Uncle
Max   & Doogie's roll is almost
gone   he's sweating   shaking   cursing his luck   thoughts of
Mona & the baby   back in the
hut   & Uncle Max just spits   & grins   strokes the dice
throws & wins

Lil & Pink Sequined Sal already in their 'van   making sweet
Mad Moloney on his milk 'n meth
perving through the crack in the door   whispering lurid
words to his other self
both of him groaning low

the kid says   *I come to join the show*
how old are you kid   says Genevie
am fifteen ma'am   looks more like twelve
come to momma   says Genevie   *I'll fix you straight*   her
mascara has run   & she wraps him up
in her satin gown   & whisks him off to her 'van   he'll be in
there till cock crow   & come out a
ruin   or maybe   a man

dosed up in the fortune teller's tent   Juicy & Bennie & Mystic
Belle   pulling on the hookah
till it's hot as hell   drifting off to dreamland   where we all
long to go   where it's all beer &
skittles   & there's no more shows

no more shows

here   wide eyed   in the shadow of night   I'm crashing in the
dirt   sweating pus & blood
in my shirt   grease paint on my face   my ears still ring   with
the blare   of the show

when I come to   there's sawdust in my hair   & nowhere
else   to go

Janet Peace

The secret of life is enjoying the passage of time, James Taylor

Janet Peace is a retired educationalist living near the spectacular North Coast of Northern Ireland. Since joining North Coast Writers, she has enjoyed the experience of sharing in the diverse creativity of the group and been encouraged and inspired by all its members. Writing jostles for position with pottering about in the garden and caring for a household of rescue cats and an old border-collie. Her large family, many pets, stunning location and reflections on life all inspire her poetry. In 2022 her poems appeared in the anthology *Love, Loss and Cardiac Issues* and in *Springboards: A Manual of Creative Writing* , both published by Impspired Press. In 2023 her poem 'The Last Dance' featured in both the Impspired Online Magazine No 21 and print edition Volume 11. Also in 2023 five of her poems featured in *Spun Tales and Woven words,* a North Coast Writers Anthology published by Impspired Press.

The Great Pottery Throw Down

The Great Potter
crafts his pots
from raw clay
clawed from earth's crust
slammed pounded kneaded
wired weighed wedged
ready for creation

some are
pinched
squeezed
simple vessels
hand-formed
crudely-moulded
humble honest
bearing makers
thumbprint

many are coiled
rolled hoops-conjoined
loops-locked ribs-rubbed
sponge - smoothed
Into circlets
of unity

others are slabbed flattened
batter-boarded angle-sharp
slipped-stuck baton-slapped
backstamp branded hard

more are
thrown
centred
firmly cupped
by caring hands
gently raised up
gripped shaped
by intuitive t
touch i
l
ceramics cremated p
cracks s
h t e
flaws s a t r

blasting kiln mates to sherds

River Walk

Passing through the kissing gate
a path sedged in season's leaves   softens our tread
gilds our route   a trove of gold   copper   bronze
foraged hazel-husks and wind-wrest pinecones
bestrew the trail   collage our prints

mottle - mossed tree stumps
display an ikebana of unfurled ferns
created by forest geisha
a rustic picket of wooden skelfs
rough-bound with twine safeguards our trek

by water's edge upended giant
brawn roots exposed   bares his soul
sculpts old man time on river's bank
gnarled tendrils snagging twigs and grass
entangle in bedraggled beard

above a preening heron
peers haughty from her perch
eyes coyly accusing
wings enfolding her breast
in a feathering of black basque

below we splash on bracken shoal
tranced by the trickle and flow
the babble   burble
the splish   splosh
river dog and I as one

Winter Warriors

squadron birds
hunker in hedge
resisting wild north-coast
hurricane blast
hopeful for just one seed
a lull in the battering
sees a rip tide flight
as epic as Earhart
as daring as Bleriot
to pick sunflower's heart
to fight the starboard list
the pendulum sway
the glacial slip-slide
of frozen feeder
for one measly mealworm
brave fragile warriors
fluffing out feathers
with ice-air to armour
gainst hailstone pepper
for just one seed

o n e
t s
s e
u e
j d

t. s
h e
a e
t d

of
survival

Giraffes and Muslin Stars

first portrait   unconfined
studying shadows   light on shade
lips tasting earthly air
we smiled at sonographic scans
embryo turned foetus
a tiny astronaut floating in space
umbilicus anchored to mother ship

now   splashed down
hair dampened in amniotic curls
skull capped by suctions pull
stork beak peck on cheek
your brow furrows in wonder
your dark eyes mirror the mystery
What do you know of giraffes
...... or of muslin stars?

Spring at Bishop's Gate

first Spring
we wandered into forest glade
brushing through herbaceous shag
of wild garlic and old-delph bluebells
shaded by boughs   serenaded by birdsong

we frog-leapt brackish bourn
counted tree-rings of thick and thin
tight-roped stone wall weir
giddy as fox cubs
heady with vulpine musk

this Spring
I stumble through relict wood
a bog garden of pungent pathos
with garlic grown rudely wild
blinding loves bell-blue eyes

I wind-chime tinkles of grief
blackboard your name in child's chalk
ache for you to hear   see   be
with me   once more
at Bishop's Gate in Spring

Sue Steging

Born and raised in Liverpool, Sue made her way south through England before settling on the banks of a small river near the Causeway Coast in Northern Ireland. After a career spanning education and psychotherapy, she is still searching for just the right words and is happy to have found a group of people engaged in that same search. Her work has been published in journals, anthologies and magazines. It can be found on the YouTube channels of The Bangor Literary Journal, Issue 11 and in the Community Arts Partnership anthologies, Heartland (2021) and Threshold (2022) where her poems, *The Goldfinch* and *a naming of parts*, were longlisted for the Seamus Heaney Award for New Writing. In 2023 she won the Seamus Heaney Award for New Writing for her poem, *Four Stories About (The Same) Crows.*

Four Stories About (The Same) Crows

I

A morning shout of crows homes in on pines I've seen
them colonise at dusk. I wonder at their energy, their
lust for this old roost. They've stripped its branches
bare.

Their black armada makes me think of refugees: of
hawks as swooping border guards chased off by
fearless crows. These birds would never, rudderless,
be humbled at the pier.

II

Crows' noisy joy turns reprimand. They tell me we are
sad land things to traffic friends, scorch earth, smash
homes to ash, make refugees.

Why not, like them, mix roosts to learn and teach new
ways, share memories, memorials, find mates?

III

Crows choose tall trees, the pine, the oak; select high forking branches for their nests, the way that human builders once picked oak and sailors chose the fir for masts.

We don't see woods that way but plant haphazard, here and there. We call trees *carbon capture* now, and hope it's for the best.

IV

Crescendo calls consensus. Time to go.

They loft their wild black sails and soar.

airborne

low enough for clouds to show me mountains villages
a river
        familiar sights   they ground me   in a sky
    the blue   of Raphael   Fra Angelico
home to cherubs   angels with rainbow wings
                heroes   heaven-bent
            (pareidolia they call it)

Speedbird   still a call sign after all these years
        smooth   streamlined   wings   give lift
(biomimicry they call it)   but metal birds take
energy
  from underground   alchemies   fomented on
innocent organisms
dead before the dinosaurs   drilled for   fought
over
          energised impatience
            (anthropocene they call it)

without its wings a plane is shuttle shaped   it
threads between
                    the warp and weft of lives
  patterning   joining
not like the old hand weavers   fingers threading   feet
pumping
  making   art   in homes that must be filled with light
         looms clattering   clacking
  this is the sound   of factories   deafening
                    deadening   for some
                            (revolution they called it)
                                                    tailspin

                    white engine noise
               sings lullaby   not sweet enough for sleep
                     but still   a dream
    knitted blankets   warm bodies   a swing
hung in a tree

                    not endings   but beginnings
  not loss   but chance regained
          the graft that roots me to the land I leave
                                              airborne

Swallows

Why do the swallows
darting back

bring memories of you?

I feel the pull
the continental drift

of lives and times
we counter
now and then

with songs to signal

as swallows do

that we still share a map.

Once we built a common nest
scooped up leftover stuff
to fill the nooks and ledges

as swallows do

then cushioned it with salvage
fabrics
feathered ornaments of the day.

It's habit now

in spring

to think of you

to trace the once familiar

flight path of our friendship

as swallows do

and share some tales

of where and how

we flew.

Samhain

clear-skied moonlight shivers
on sleeping ground
Arcturus shares its traveller's light
above the oak

the tree lets wind
unstopped by leaves
blow through
I hear it sough

branches creak and flex
as sap withdraws into the core
bark hardens
in seasonal retreat

the oak makes ready
for coming shocks of frost
cherishing the future
showing us the way

Secret Boxes

I

Once upon a time, at the edge of a small town, itself on the edge of a large and neglected tract of ancient woodland, an old carpenter waited out his days. It was not by accident that his many journeys had brought him to rest here. He needed plenty of space between himself and other people. People who, for instance, would call him the old carpenter when he considered himself to be the maestro of the art of working in wood. He could not become numb to the disappointments that came to be inherent in the pursuit of his art. They generated quite a cloud around him and so he was best left alone until he moved on. No one was sad to see him go.

He had spent some time in Japan, blown there by the harsh winds that drove the British Navy. Even at sea, some jack of all trades would amuse himself by mocking a man who chose to spend his hours off-watch, sober, embellishing the oak of the mast and capstan, allowing the beauty of the grain to come to the surface and nourish his own wooden heart as it had nourished the living tree before it had been given to this god-forsaken task of murder and mayhem in the service of an unbearably ugly commerce.

In Japan he had freed himself from this incongruous joining of tree and ocean. He managed to find a place on the outskirts of the imperial court. Excluded from full access through race and custom, he was gratified to find his talent recognised and appreciated. As well as new skills, he learned about the ways of such a court: the intrigue, forbidden intimacies and their consequences, ambition, above all, ambition and ultimately assassination. As an outsider he had his uses: his childless mentor passed on the secret skills he learned so well that he was accepted as *myadaiku*; a full acknowledgement of his skills. Without the prejudices of the local craftsmen he was able to apply those skills to bring to the courtiers the new fashion for *Himitsu Bako*, ornately decorated boxes for the keeping of valuables, and valuable secrets . And he applied older skills to ensure that, at a price, there might be unwelcome surprises in store for those who tried to pry.

But life had taught him nothing of acceptance and gratitude: he only knew rivalry and he thought to deal with the ambiguities of his position by turning against his master, using the poison his master had taught him to make. In his preoccupation with the wood, he had misread the culture. Hard as it was to acknowledge that his envied master had also been his mentor and protector, he was brought to realise that those who bought his luxurious and sometimes deadly boxes, cabinets and domestic art works would only do so through his trusted intermediary. He was left in the shadows. They grew deeper. He was forced to move on.

Increasingly bitter, he found more and more patrons for the art of the deadly and subtle poisons: embedded in the most innocent of domestic artefacts, attractive and functional enough to be touched frequently, or designed to be opened by intricate manoeuvres, they could pave the way to a sleep of a thousand hours, and no-one woke from that. He learned how to place the chosen poison on a splinter so delicate that its entry into the flesh would hardly be noticed.

Eventually he settled on the edge of the remote woodland and practiced his dark arts in solitude. When contracts were scarce he found his own victims in those who had disappointed him in the past and made passing phantoms of the human contacts that remained to him.

When his own end finally came it was, as might be expected, unremarked for some time. Eventually, the undertaker and his assistant came to the house to do the grisly business of seeing to the desiccated remains of a figure upright in his chair as though on a throne. Around the walls, densely packed and leaving only room for a door and a high window for illumination were stacks of shelves filled with marvels of his art. Oak, beech, walnut, rosewood, ebony they could recognise but many woods they had never seen before. Each piece was inlaid with the most marvellous decorations in other rare woods or with mother of pearl, ivory, even crystal and moonstone; some were lacquered and speckled with gold in the Japanese fashion.

The Mayor of the town, for there was no other to lay claim to this treasure, ordered them off to auction in the city, mentally listing as he did so all the improvements to be provided for the people of a town the unhappy benefactor had so deeply despised.

And so, in the richest quarter of the richest city, there came to be an auction. A rich lord sent his man of business with a free hand to bid for an interesting collection of bibelots with which to furnish the boudoir of his new wife.

II

On reflection it was not mere accident that the man of business, well aware of his master's proclivities, should have assisted in furnishing the wife's private space with boxes, however beautiful and artistic. Constraint of a different order followed her into the bedchamber. And not surprising either perhaps that while her eyes were wet, her womb was dry. Tiring of this, Milord increased the intensity of his demands. Her state was an affront to him and she was unfit to be seen in public until her duty was done, while in private she was to be available to him at all times.

Invitations, at first submitted to Milady for polite refusal were soon to be refused at the door until finally they were withdrawn. Letters from her distant family were admitted until one day Milord appeared with one of her replies. Carefully phrased and the tearstains visible only to the educated eye, it was still too revealing. But letters must be sent, else visitors might appear. She learned to write and take refuge in the sweetest of epistles, full of pretty dresses, (seen in the street), sparkling evening parties (seen in retrospect) and elegant tea parties with imaginary friends. Her sobs she saved for the silent nights. Meanwhile, letters containing the truth of the limitations of her prison and its miseries were also written, addressed carefully and stored in the pretty boxes with which she was now so familiar and which she had learned to open with great care. Strange that those lovely smooth boxes should have such prickly catches when first opened.

And still, in spite of all attempts, following many scientific theories firmly applied, the wife failed to do her duty. Other means of securing the succession must be found. Milord withdrew to test his options farther afield, sympathy for his sad plight as the husband of a woman perhaps not long for this world gaining him entry to salons which might otherwise be closed to him.

As he withdrew, so did the servants. Her own maid, sent with her trousseau, had long returned to the country in an apparent act of generosity, to counter potential homesickness. The staff who replaced her understood their role well and with little to do except oil the locks and maintain minimum hygiene, they spent much of their time in the Butler's parlour, availing of the extra delicacies that they amassed through filching her small allowance. Eventually, their usage of her became more unkind. They spoke loudly and in her hearing of her husband's new conquest, the jewels he had bought, the silks and satins he had them deliver.

Her letters continued to gather but her use of paper was monitored as it cut into the profits of her jailers. It was unreasonable that the letters she was still required to send should require so much paper and ink. There were no papers to be collected; no spoiled drafts seemed to be burned in her meagre fires. They joked about increasing her rations (although they never did). She must be hungry, they laughed if she had turned to eating paper.

As interest fell away and the household developed new rhythms around her, it became too much of a chore to see to the locks and all the extra work that entailed. She began to drift through the rooms at night in the silence that had become habitual. In search of the paper that had become her only correspondent she finally found the courage to enter her husband's study. A place of soft luxury compared to her own rooms, the large desk strewn with papers betraying the interest he still had in managing the large estates that his marriage had secured for him. There were stocks of paper and ink enough to pillage in secrecy. Eventually, realizing that the servants had become a self-sufficient society below stairs, she allowed her curiosity to take her further and she began, carefully and quietly, to begin a nightly exploration of the writing in his cabinets. She found much to inform her own recordings.

III

One day, as she was sitting in her habitual seat just back from her window, she heard an unfamiliar tread in the corridor and the door suddenly opened. Her husband was there, smiling. "Look what I have brought you. I found another box by the man who made the others. I thought I would bring it to you. I see you like them. They are cleaner than anything else in the room. Including yourself, now I come to look at you." His smile dimmed. He seemed surprised by her calm silence. He expressed dissatisfaction with her hair and dress. "What am I paying that woman for?" But then, calmer, he asked about her health. "You are damnably thin and pale", he said, "but I suppose…"He straightened his shoulders. "Well here is another pretty box for your collection. I believe it has a secret drawer. You can amuse yourself trying to open it. But don't wait too long, the surprise is perishable."

But her time in the room with her boxes had taught her more than one secret of their maker's skill. She knew that the boxes' designs were as devious and as subtle as an assassin could make them. She realized that another must know their ways as she did and was prepared to look for the sharpness to be navigated enroute to the secret drawers. And in this case she had been warned that the trap was live.

So carefully, and wearing the strongest gloves to be found in her depleted wardrobe, she began to search for the box's secret. And there it was. A needle this time, disturbingly sharp with an opalescent tip and a scent of almonds. The apprentice seemed less than subtle but no less effective for that. Just as carefully, she replaced the parts, leaving only the needle to hand.

By this time the servants were all deep in their drunken and complacent sleep. Her husband had also stayed at home this night. She didn't need to wonder why but it made her doubly cautious as she crept into his study; found his pen, his ink, his paper and copying a long familiar hand, wrote a sweet letter. " My darling, a sweet surprise for you to break your fast. Sealed with a loving kiss." And she signed it with the name of the old school friend who was now the recipient of her husband's favours.

She took the letter and the needle to the kitchen. Going to the Butler's private pantry she found the special conserve her sweet-toothed husband enjoyed and dipped the point of the needle in it, leaving it for a moment to ensure that all its essence had been absorbed. She left the note on the early morning tray, hoping that the servants would each assume a late delivery and not dare to interfere with that letter writer.

And then she returned to her room, to wait with her boxes and the spirit of their maker, wondering if her old self, the one she had entrusted to the letters in her own secret boxes, would find a place in the world when the door was opened.

Rhona Stephens

Born in Northern Ireland, Rhona Stephens divides her time between Scotland's Royal Deeside and Ireland's Causeway Coast. She enjoys writing poetry and prose, drawing inspiration from the natural world and her Christian faith. In 2023, she was short listed for the Wells Festival of Literature Open Poetry Competition and long listed for The Rialto Nature and Place Poetry Competition. Her work has appeared in Irish Hares and Seahorses and Love, Loss and Cardiac Matters, published by Impspired Press, 2022; in Spun Yarns and Woven Words, Impspired Press, 2023; and on Retreat West website. Her children's poems have appeared in The Toy magazine and on The Dirigible Balloon and Charles Causley Trust websites.

A fistful of feathers

close-wrapped   we stand
scarce breathing
lest even frosty exhalation
should abort his landing

birds small as eggcups
come and go

at coffee call he lights
we lean in to the wall
become still-life
not wanting him to stall

poised for flight
he flits   branch to branch to branch
to feeder
a fistful of feathers   that's all
but oh   his beauty
re-joys our souls
gilds our day

as we stand   close-wrapped
scarce breathing

a poet's guide to punctuation

common speech marks and their friends have served their purpose met their ends
no need for them so you can drop the semicolon and full stop

always stifle the temptation to use marks of exclamation
and colons in a poem today are not considered quite au fait

the modern poet likes white space
to punctuate will bring disgrace
or at the very least a sigh and murmurs of quaint times gone by

note if you want to win a prize you need to catch the judges' eyes
do not use a curly comma or you'll cause those judges trauma
then you can kiss goodbye to fame with only your sweet self to blame
for I have warned you
as I said the punctuation mark is
d
e
a
d

The Great Divide

A soft skiff of early evening rain cooled the village hall. Outside only. Inside, nothing could lower the temperature of a hall filled with overheated teenagers.

Boys, determinedly casual in dress and manner, lounged against one wall, sneaking glances across the way at girls whose bold fashion statements were a cover story. Inside, we were naive as a baby's blanket.

The band was incidental. Only the drum was significant, becoming our collective heartbeat, accelerating, intensifying, palpitating as the evening wore on.

My tangerine cord pinafore was a daring four inches above the knee and much admired by friends.

Before ever his eye caught mine, I knew he would ask. I turned my back on him as he crossed the great divide, pleaded in vain for my friend to drag me away.

"Would you like to dance?" he asked, all courtesy and cleanliness in his pressed shirt and polished shoes.

His courage in crossing the hall eluded me then. His humiliation in having to return alone haunts me still.

Beyond

If I were to say I am coping, that would be true. I have made it here, to this island beyond an island. And I am free. Hitching the backpack onto one shoulder, laptop case onto the other, I stand listening to the silence that is not a silence, for it is brim full of the sighs of summer and the soft sounds of the sea. And something else. There… Ebbing and flowing at the whim of an air current, I hear it one last time. The faint put-put-put of Jackie Muir's boat as he makes his way back to the big island.

A disappointing trip Jackie had, for I was not a communicative passenger. And I was his only passenger. He was eager to ask questions I was unwilling to answer. Questions he will be asked when he returns to the harbour, for I saw curiosity in the eyes of those men outside the Douglas Arms this morning. I could almost taste the questions on the tongue tip of the woman who served me at the store. Questions, too, from the owner of the Airbnb where I stayed last night. Yes, there will be questions for Jackie Muir when he gets back, but he will have no answers.

There are no cars on the island, one of the reasons I chose to come here. I follow the sun east to west, making my way on foot up the gravel path that slices the island in two. Reaching what I calculate to be an approximate midpoint, I pause for a drink. A seal-grey rock provides a perfect shelf on which to rest the backpack. My water bottle is already lukewarm, for the temperature has risen quickly this morning, with the wind no more than a whisper in the gorse.

Scanning the sparse landscape, I stifle a moment's panic, wondering if I have chosen wisely. Easier, perhaps, to hide in a city than seek sanctuary in an environment where every movement attracts the eyes of every resident. Even the non-human ones, I realise, as every sheep in sight views me with an uneasy mix of curiosity and caution.

I can be of little interest to them for long. All they see is a middle-aged man, indistinguishable from other occasional hikers who make it this far west. Nothing shows on the outside. Nothing. Except perhaps a wariness in my eyes and deep vertical lines from nose to chin making me look older than my two score and seven. But sheep pay no heed to that.

Transferring the backpack to the springy turf at my feet, I sit on the rock and consider to where I have come. The landscape rises and falls, but it does so with a half-heartedness that gives the whole place the tame look of a duvet on an unmade bed. Nowhere does the land rise to a majestic peak. No brooding spine of hills commands the centre or creates a barrier round the coast. I see squat shrubs and a scattering of stunted native trees, steeply slanted by prevailing winds. And to the south and east, juvenile plantings of commercial conifers. Indeed, the whole island gives the impression of suppressed adolescence, of nothing and nowhere being allowed to reach its full potential.

I listen again to the silence that is not a silence. As I swallow another mouthful of water, my eyes track a muted cry to a circling red kite. What prey has his keen eye spotted? Or is he just reminding them, with his ridiculous mewing, that he is here, that he can target and take them any time he chooses? I feel for those hapless, hidden creatures, feel for them with the empathy of one who has lived long within the sightline of those who would destroy him.

The croft surprises me. I anticipated a building by the shore or facing me on a hillside, positioned so we could get to know one another from a distance before meeting face to face. Instead, *Comraich* lies low in the crook of the western bay, set back from the shoreline, concealing its existence till I leave the main path and begin the gentle descent to sea level.

The key is exactly where Hector McConnell said it would be. It lies warm in my hand, almost the full length of it, and turns with surprising ease in the oversized keyhole. I nudge the door open with my knee, navigating both body and backpack into the room.

No amount of polish or air freshener can disguise that smell peculiar to old cottages, a unique essence of inadequate damp-proofing and ineffective ventilation. I inhale the dead air and exhale slowly, a long breath that sets dust motes dancing along a slash of sunlight slanting through the sash window.

Retired beneath dust sheets, a couple of armchairs shrink into the corners either side of the hearth. On the shadowed side of the room, a bed. A single bed for a single room to eat, sleep and live in, with the contemporary convenience of WiFi and a shower room. It is enough. All I will need.

I spend the rest of the day familiarising myself with the idiosyncrasies of the croft, discovering that if I leave the front door open the bathroom door will slam-crack shut, sharp as a pistol shot. The cold tap in the kitchen drips slow enough to deceive me into thinking it has stopped, only to begin again just as my nerves relax into the silence.

If I sit at the table by the window, I have a clear view of the shoreline. Views in other directions are limited, either because of the size and placement of windows or, at the rear, because the wall is windowless.

My afternoon is spent unpacking equipment from the backpack, setting up surveillance cameras and alarms. Everything is linked to laptop and phone. Despite the remoteness of the island, Hector has done well, for the signal and download speed is excellent. I go to bed, having seen no-one, and sleep surprisingly well, knowing I have made the croft, or rather made myself as safe as possible.

At 4.37am I am woken by the security alarm. It is already an hour since dawn and Hector McConnell is on his way. Standing on the threshold of the croft, I hear him long before I see him.

Guide me, O thou great Redeemer,
Pilgrim through this barren land…

Rich and deep, his voice arrives before him, just as it did when I first met him over twenty years ago on the rigs, where his habit of hymn-singing earned him the nickname 'Holy Hector'. His faith was as deep as his voice and we teased him shamelessly about both. But there wasn't one of us who was not glad to have Hector on our shift, singing *We have an anchor that keeps the soul steadfast and sure as the billows roll* when an alarm bell rang, or a massive mid-winter storm hammered our rig a hundred miles off the coast of Aberdeen.

Rounding the corner of the croft, Hector comes to a standstill directly in front of me. For a full minute, I reckon, we do not speak.

"Well lad," he says, finally, "it's good to see you."

I nod, not trusting my voice. Stepping forward, I take the rucksack as he slides it off his shoulder. He looks me over from head to foot.

"I wouldn't have known you if I'd met you on the road."

"Good."

"I got everything you asked for, but you'll need to empty this rucksack, for I'll have to take it back with me for next time."

I unpack the rucksack, then scramble some eggs while Hector toasts bread and makes a pot of tea. We sit across the table from each other, eating our 5am breakfast in silence.

When we've finished, Hector pours us each another mug of tea and motions me outside.

Taking a seat on an old wooden bench under the front window, it occurs to me that, in different circumstances, this could be the beginning of an idyllic island holiday. As if reading my thoughts, Hector turns to me.

"Ethan, lad, you're here to work. So we'd better get you clued up on what you'll need to know and what you'll be doing."

I finish the tea and set the mug on the bench beside me.

"Ready."

Hector stands a while before moving, allowing flexibility to return to stiffened limbs.

"Ah, this arthritis fair slows me down. No one's surprised I'm taking on a man to help. Though they'd be surprised to hear I'm hiring a novice!"

His smile fades as he continues.

"If this is going to work, Ethan, it has to look real. No, it has to become real. You have to become Ethan MacQuoid, stockman. The few folk staying on the island and the handful that, like myself, have land they look to now and again, are no bampots. They'll see through any blether and bluster."

"I know. I know," I repeat.

"Right, well let's find out how much you do know."

The cattle are already grazing the salt marsh grasses and take little notice as we head towards them.

"Good land, is it?" Hector asks, with a nod toward the hill behind the croft.

"No. Rushes and bracken. And a lot of water. There could be good grazing but it hasn't been managed properly. The Highland cattle will help improve that."

"Why Highland?"

"They're lighter than other breeds and don't trample the ground into a mud swamp. They can cope with the weather. You've got a fold of fifty, one bull for breeding. Bullocks butchered at four years old, twice as old as more commercial beef. And they graze a variety of species, not just grass. That, and the seaweed they eat at low tide, gives them great flavour… And gives you premium price for the carcasses," I add, giving him a sideways glance as he comes to a standstill.

Hector laughs. "So you did read the stuff I sent. Well remembered. It's basic, but it is a start, lad, just in case you come across someone before you get the hang of things yourself. Now, come on. You've got a lot to learn. Come and meet the girls and Dougal Dubh."

We spend the morning with the cattle and sheep, Hector explaining, me taking notes. A quick midday dinner of mince and tatties and we are out again, this time to the rear of the croft where a fence has to be repaired. It is past five o'clock by the time we head back indoors for a quick cup of tea before Hector leaves.

He is seated at the table, making a list of jobs for me when a succession of rifle shots whip-cracks through the air. Disoriented as a spinning penny, I sink to the ground, voiceless, sweating, the mug of tea I'm carrying fragmented on the floor beside me.

Hector lays a firm hand on my shoulder to steady me.

"Come on, lad. That's just some Jock shooting rabbits. Come on, now. No-one's coming, no-one's here. It's over."

But it isn't over. Not in my head. Not in my heart. Not when everything I lived for and everyone I loved is gone.

"It'll never be over, Hector."

Taking his hand off my shoulder, Hector sighs into the silence before speaking again.

"No, lad, I reckon you're right. But we have to find a way of living alongside our sorrows. Come on, now, sit up at the table. There's another mug of tea in the pot."

I mop up the spilt drink and wrap the broken mug in packing paper.

Breaking open a pack of biscuits, Hector tips a handful on a plate and sets them before me.

"I'll stay the night and keep you company."

He brushes aside my protest.

"I'll stay the night," he repeats, and it is settled.

Like a starting pistol, those shots trigger the memory track to my past, to that night I got home and came face to face with a killer. The night I found my wife and two daughters limp and lifeless. The night I, who would have given my life for them, found myself under suspicion of taking their lives.

Hector makes sandwiches and a fresh pot of tea and we take them outside to the bench. We eat and talk till the sun sets. And then keep talking till it rises again. Talk about things Hector already knows, for it seems important, somehow, that my story is established here, absorbed into the fabric of this new place. That I am known for who I really am in this environment where I am seeking sanctuary.

We talk of that first night, of the court case and my conviction and sentencing and imprisonment. Of the retrial and release. Of the subsequent attempts on my life that persuaded the authorities finally, finally to believe what I had said from the beginning. And to provide me with a new identity. New documents, new name, new life. None of which, of course, can erase the old. None of which is a salve for the complexities of grief.

"He's still there, Hector."

"And you're still here, Ethan. And with God's help we're going to build you a new future."

"I wish I had your faith."

"That may come, Ethan, that may come. You can't live long among these islands without knowing you're part of something greater and grander than yourself. And after all you've been through, you surely know there's more to the heart of a man than can be explained by science and circumstance."

I say nothing, knowing his convictions will not be shaken by anything I might say. Besides, he may just be right. I have seen in the heart of man that which cannot be explained by nature or nurture. Science is only part of the truth. There is more beyond and Hector's explanation is as good as any I've heard. Better than most, indeed. It has made of him the kindest man I have known, a man who is now putting his life at risk to help me.

The lives of his cattle, too, I remember, rising as I hear them call an early morning greeting one to another.

"I'd better see to the stock," I say, and he nods.

"I'll give you a hand before I go."

If I were to say I am coping, that would be partially true. I am here. I have made it to this island beyond an island. Still, I am not free. Not free from danger, not free from grief, not free from memories. They cast a long shadow over the past. And over the future.

But as I sit here on the bench, listening to Hector hymn-singing his way home, looking out on the view he considers to be the brightest jewel in God's creation, I think I may have chosen wisely after all and found a suitable place and companion for this strange new life. Experience leaves me with little expectation of justice, but perhaps, in time, I can find a way to live alongside my sorrows.

Denise Ellis

Having lived and worked on the North Coast of Northern Ireland for thirty-five years, Denise presently lives in the seaside town of Portstewart. Since joining Sanderlings Creative Writing Group in the Spring of 2023, and encouraged by the other Group Members, she has found herself writing ever since. Always interested in the natural world, especially in birds, Nature and the stunning landscape where she lives influence inspires her writing.

Devil Birds

Summering
Screaming
Screeching
Sultry solstice
Siren call
Summiting
Swooping
Sweeping
Satanic Sickle
Sheering Sky
Stretching
Swiftlings
Swansong
Southering
Soaring Away

Footnote: *Mysterious and enigmatic, Swifts were known in history and folklore as devil birds, thought to hibernate in mud with screaming calls which were the cries of damned human souls on their way to hell. Migrating from Africa, spending just three summer months in Europe, they eat, sleep and mate on the wing only landing to breed, nesting in tiny cracks high up in buildings. 2015. With a red UK conservation status which means they are globally threatened, Swift populations in the UK and Ireland have declined by 51 % between 1995 and 2015. More information can be found at swift-conservation.org*

Interment

Soft grey rain fell on the couple working side by side

hoods up against the elements

heads down intent on their task

She cradled a small swaddled form   he held a spade

Do you think that's deep enough?

Maybe go down a bit more   there's a fox around here

It

was

done

He bowed his head   a solitary tear dropped to the cool earth

Night night   sleep tight, he whispered

They turned to face each other

tentative arms outstretched for comfort

Thanks   thanks for helping

That's alright, son   she was a special cat

IN THE SOUP

The summer I left school was memorable. Six unsettled weeks until exam results would determine my next steps in life. I whiled away the days ,a supermarket job, hung out with friends, and visited my Grandmother.

A self-absorbed teenager I was unaware of longstanding and regular gatherings at granny's house.
My mother and aunts, unencumbered by children, husbands, partners, would meet for lunch and a conflab. That summer I was welcomed to the feminine inner circle of the family

Granny was independent, longer a widow than a wife . Outspoken , mischievous ,with a penchant for extravagant headwear . Underlying her more exuberant qualities was a kind and generous heart.

During my childhood my aunts provided a welcoming play place complete with cousins and sustenance when required . At granny's away from their domestic circles they revealed themselves anew. They arrived in a flurry of chat and laughter ,recounting their mornings work. Short skirts, knee length boots, Silvikrin hair ,a shimmer of lipstick. The air around them was sometimes blue (John Player No 6) the odd expletive punctuating a racy story.
I was in awe of their glamour and confidence

My Mum my constant

Granny was a great cook and home baker ,I eagerly anticipated lunch . My favourite was her soup. Familiar comforting unique to this place
Silken stock Shin of beef, simmered until melting off the bone
A trio of tender pulses
Dew fresh vegetables plucked from the garden .
A handful of vibrant parsley to finish
Ladled over a floury spud , affection in a bowl.

I had enjoyed a few mouthfuls when I put my spoon down ,I didn't know where to look . Maternal telepathy alerted, my mum mouthed *what's wrong*? I pointed into my bowl . She considered the myriad tiny green bodies masquerading as parsley , put a finger to her lips *Shhh* .
Poured the remains into her bowl and continued to eat .
Granny appeared from the kitchen brandishing a teapot .*My goodness pet , you must be very hungry, would you like some …….*
My stomach flipped ………*apple tart.*
Relief having restored my appetite I had two huge slices ,Granny was delighted .

Despite the S word hanging in the air, the afternoon continued as usual ,easy conversation and anecdote supported by cups of tea and cake .

Some Years Later

A special family meal hosted by a favorite uncle. The starter arrives. Whole king prawns, beady bemused eyes , shell and tentacles intact. Across the table my thirteen year old daughter meets my gaze ……I know what I have to do.

I still make Grannys soup.
When I'm washing parsley with meticulous intent, I remember
An indomitable Grandmother
Spirited Aunts
A gentle mother
My teenaged self , the summer I left home for Higher Education .

CORNCRAKE

Clinging to the edge
Of life   last refuge
Rockfaced islands   West
North   winding tight   an ancient clock
CREX
        CREX
Recall time past
Abundant hayfields   long   lush
Knapweed   Yarrow   Meadow Brown
Elusive   summer   lullaby

Footnote:

Corncrakes, with their distinctive call from which they get their onomatopoeic scientific name Crex Crex, are often heard during summer nights though rarely seen as these secretive birds nest and keep low in long meadow grass. No longer familiar in Ireland, the Corncrake is now restricted to a few stronghold areas, Tory Island in Donegal, Rathlin Island off the North Coast and in West Connaught, their decline linked to C20th agricultural change, most notably the switch from hay meadows to early cut silage .

Beachcomber

~ after George Mackay Brown ~

Monday   I found a spade   small
upstanding   seaweed bound
I carried it home
plaything for a child

Tuesday   a fish box washed overboard
new life   on land
next Spring
a planter for beans

Wednesday   the sea gods smile
Gannets shout   treasure
TREASURE   a wishing stone
a hag stone   mermaids tears
Quahog   Groatie Buckie
Palmful of shells

Thursday   cast off cola can
Coffee cup   chocolate wrapper
fissling on the sand
picnic over   Dunlins cry

Friday   stubbed out butts defile the shore
taint of smoke sours

the soft sea air
cinder fragments underfoot
last remains a midnight pyre

Saturday foul green bag discreetly tucked
out of sight between two rocks
out of mind
Bucky bottle breaches waves lost
found where dolphins play

Sunday fearing interlopers
I go to the ocean early
What's Heaven? an empty beach
a cowrie shell

Pamela Leetch

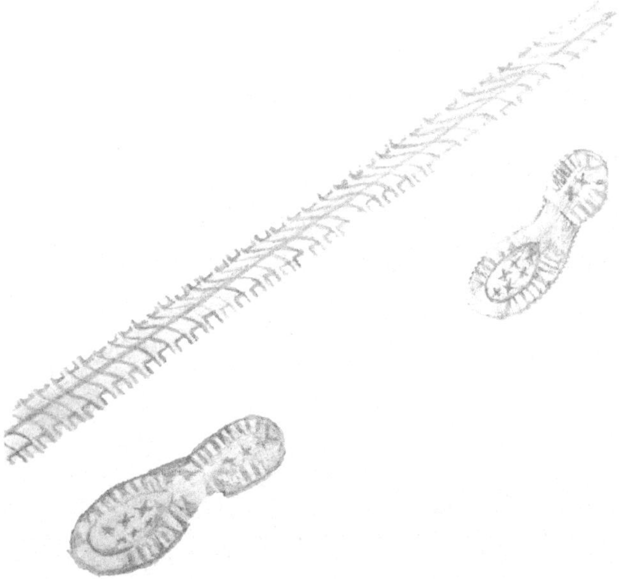

Born and raised in Ballymena, Northern Ireland, Pamela Leetch spent her adult working life in England. During that time she maintained her roots through family bonds and an enduring love for her birthplace. Now returned to live in Portstewart, Northern Ireland, scene of many a happy holiday, she is a member of the Sanderlings Creative Writing Group in which she has begun to write about her roots and explore her love of the written word in all its forms.

I Remember I Remember

(After Thomas Hood and Philip Larkin)

I remember I remember the house where I was born
twenty-five homes jammed tight together neighbours chatting
over the whitewashed front garden walls linking our lives
friendships made neighbours lost the flow of life
clear from the very beginning

I remember I remember the house where I was born
inter-connected back gardens Alsatian dogs roaming free
watching them jump the garden gates not afraid
as they got closer and closer my mother lifting me out of their way
me crying because I liked the look and the feel of them

I remember I remember the house where I was born
monday morning wash boiled up in the old steel boiler
steaming up windows
helping my mother with the mangle turning the wheel
careful of my fingers
standing beside her as she pinned the sheets to the line rain or shine,
a sense of achievement then dinner warm Watch with Mother

I remember   I remember   the house where I was born
steps up from the street to the green front door   it felt so high
standing with her   waving to the riders on their way to the stables
seeing the students walk by   their uniform duffel coats and scarves
offering a glimpse of a future still all mine to take

I remember, I remember, the house where I was born
the hiss of hot iron on wet cloth   me under the table enveloped
in a Winter Wonderland   the smell of my father's cigarettes mingling with
the smell of smoke from coal fires on wet winter evenings walking home
with the two of them   stars
hands held   the
swinging   beneath
                                            up

High Heel Heaven

All her life she had wanted to be over six feet tall. She was above average height anyway, but that was never quite enough. On seeing those shoes with their six-inch heel in the very exclusive shop she passed every day on her way to work, she just knew they were meant for her. She tried them on. They felt fabulous … and so did she. She knew exactly when and where she would wear them. The Annual May Lunch for the staff of the offices of Drake, Drake and Bichon, Holborn Solicitors, where she worked as a conveyancer.

She intended to make an entrance. On the day of the lunch, wearing trainers into the office, she changed into the shoes just before leaving for the nearby restaurant. As her feet hit the pavement she felt her body freeze. Although willing her feet to move, the dynamic between the contact of the heels on the cement and the angle of the heels just would not let her move. The beautiful shoes had to come off, be replaced with her very ordinary trainers.

Not the entrance she had intended but noticed by everyone nonetheless.

A Cat called Alice

A malevolent cat sits on my head. Her name is Alice. For the most part she keeps her claws retracted her fury under control. Cats can be unpredictable. They give the impression of being disinterested often a little morose. Alice, in fact, can channel many human emotions. This is quite unusual even disturbing in its implications. Anyway, for now she sits quiet on my head her soft paws tucked under her tail curled round her body in a very efficient and pleasing manner.

Alice and I have been together for as long as I can remember. I am nearly seventy so that makes her incredibly old. Thanks to modern diets and medications cats can live to a good age these days. I often wonder if they are happy to just sit around existing because their human guardians decree it to be the best thing. Still, you'd be surprised to know just how many cats like Alice are around. Sitting silent maybe with an occasional low purr or maybe a growl but mostly silent with one ear half-cocked always always listening.

Alice hears things before there is anything to hear. She anticipates, then reacts to keep herself safe. By extension that keeps me safe too.. She is my lookout my security guard. She guards me well even when I do not need or want to be guarded or kept safe. At the first sign of anything out of the ordinary she slowly moves into action. I am grateful for that at least because if she sprang into action I think I may have a heart attack. Her ears go back. Her eyes flash emerald, green, such a pretty colour in her case it signals all systems go. And, indeed, all the systems do go.

I am never quite sure what will spring her trap, sometimes it might be a smell or a sound but, as she is a cat and I do not speak cat, I can never work it out. And she is malevolent. By that I mean she seems to enjoy the chaos which follows that flash of emerald, green, pressing down on my scalp hitting all the appropriate pressure points. Unless I am standing in front of a mirror I cannot see what she is doing. For that reason, among others, I avoid mirrors most of the time. However, I imagine her as a cartoon cat, fur on end her claws digging into my scalp as she throws her head back howls in ecstasy.

That howl. My skin prickles. My heart races. My breathing speeds up to the point where I feel I might faint. The pattern is relentless. It plays out to the end in the same way each time. Every organ in my body strives towards escape and freedom. I am depleted at the end of each cycle exhausted yet so relieved.

The first time it happened, I was so young, I thought I would die. The next time, I was a little older, I knew I would die. Now I am resigned to the fact that I *won't* die because of Alice. I still haven't worked out how to live with her. Thankfully, it happens less as I get older because Alice is older too. Her claws are less sharp. The howl, however, is still as powerful. Sometimes it represents a cannonade of frustration, a full brass section of the orchestra. Sometimes a foghorn of despair.

Some people with cats on their heads call it Anxiety. I prefer to call her Alice.

Footsteps in the Sand

Four hundred million years ago two lands collided
seas tamed
mountains formed
Opposites attracted brought together by the Continental Drift
bone grating on bone
sideways on
Our world constantly shifting changing while we evolved from
walking upright
bacterial specks to
Trekking from birthplace to the far corners of the earth
survival in violence
blind exploration
Spellbound in amber fantastical fossils dusty shards
joyful finds
drinking vessels
Tapping into collective memories of diverse histories
nose to tail
following on
Emulating absorbing the strength of those who walked ahead
straight
firm steps never lines
Praising in song praying to many supreme beings
wooden crosses
standing stones
Settling down on this island at the edge of the world
cultivating gardens
growing crops

I walk the land they walked   I breathe the air they breathed
genes   DNA
forever connected
No looking back   striving to forge ahead
follow the arrow
honour the legacy
Tribal colours accepted   rejected   marching on
Lambeg drums
flute bands
Hearts beat in unison with the rhythm of marching feet
future unknown
remembered past
Evening birdsong soars over a backdrop of tanks
Sirens   soldiering on
tarred in trauma
Spirits of our ancestors   quaking   howling like wolves
healing   soothing
nature's pools
Alternative paths offering   clarity   murk   for our future
our choice
our descendants
Next turn in the road could be the last   or   maybe   the first
one step at a time
just make the choice
Determined   I walk on   my footprints in the sand point forward
into the abyss
dark
light
no turning back

Happy Families

I came across this photograph when helping my mother move house. It's of my family Mother Father my brother and me. As I recall it was a photograph taken by the local newspaper as we were one of the first families in our area to have a television set. Father never let us forget this fact. There we are all smiles sitting transfixed by something on the set. The central point of our evening at that time was after we had eaten tea. Mother had cleared up everything washed and put away in the way my parents decreed. It was only then that we would all sit together and watch the television. I have no recollection of what was on. It all seemed magical at the time but what's on now seems mainly rubbish to me.

After thirty minutes we would be sent off to bed. Then the shouting began. To this day I cannot sit with others watching TV without that sense of impending doom. It is only now that he is dead that I can say out loud that our father hit our mother. We had to listen to the sounds of it with TV jingles jangling in our heads.

My brother and I never spoke of it then. We still don't.

Mother doesn't watch television at all now.
She listens to the radio.

Brendan Magee

From Garrison Co. Fermanagh, Northern Ireland, Brendan currently lives in Coleraine. A retired civil servant, his career chain started in London and included Belfast, Bootle (Merseyside), Manchester and finally Coleraine. A member of Sanderlings, he enjoys writing mainly prose, occasionally some poetry. His Performance pieces include *McGarrigle's Field,* a play for Big Telly Drama Club performed 25th March 2015 in Flowerfield Art Centre Portstewart, Northern Ireland, *Branch Minutes and Me and Helen Mirren* for the BBC Radio Ulster programme Time of Our Lives, 2017, and *Living Up To The Name* for Orchard Flash Festival in Armagh, 2019 , available on YouTube. Among his published Prose pieces are *Living Up To The Name* , as above , published in The Bramley Anthology, vol 2., 1917, and *The Ring* in Flash Fiction Magazine, 2019. Two of his poems have been published in Community Arts Partnership Anthologies; *Carlo's Island* in *Resonance,* 2018 and *The Last Sense* in *Find,* 2019.

What 's in a name

Hi Will. How are things in St Ratford.

It's Stratford.

St Ratford, Stratford. What's in a name.

Twenty pounds if you're selling your house.

What, are you moving?

Yeah, Anne hath her way. We are moving to London.

Oh, I suppose you might as well. You spend most of your time down here.

We are going to rent a house in Covent Garden.

What have you got for me this time. A play?

Yes.

I hope it's not one of those about beating the hell out of the French. You know the new King has French relatives. And I don't want one with a load of fairies and sprites. Tights cost a fortune these days. Oh, and that reminds me. I need to up my fee.

What! You already take eighty-five per cent.

Most of the big agents in London are taking over ninety.

What are you doing for the extra money?

What am I doing! Who gets you on at the Globe? Do you think it is only a matter of clicking my fingers? I have to bung the manager a fistful every time. Then I have to deal with the ABS.

Who?

The ABS, Anyone but Shakespeare. Ben, John and the boys have written to the Lord Chamberlain complaining that you are monopolising productions. I had to promise him a lead role for his son in all future plays. And then CWAW.

What's that? A tax?

No. Cast Women As Women. My sister says she hasn't had a role since 1594 when she was the back of the horse of Richard 111. You write these female roles, but they end up being played by men. Well the women picketed the last production of Romeo and Juliet. I must admit they had a point. Mickey Butcher playing Juliet. He's six foot and twenty stone at least. I had to pay for four walk ons to prop up the balcony when he was on.

But all productions use men to play female roles.

Things are changing Will. You'll find that when you move down permanently. Besides you can save money. Women are paid less. A play in cockney? If you need someone to write any music I can ask my cousins Charles and Davide.

No, it's the story of a rabbit who eats deadly nightshade, wakes up as a human on the moon surrounded by deer which are half white, half black. They're actually Greek gods who spend the play turning into Roman Emperors … apart from the rabbit which becomes a turkey.

Yeah, sounds like a turkey to me. Look I have an idea. You haven't written about the Irish or a play set in Ireland. The King is keen to establish good relations with the Irish. He has just licensed a distillery in Bushmills in the north of the country.

Mm, you're giving me an idea. I could write about women working there. Have them dancing round a vat.

Fine, fine as long as there's no leprechauns. We can't afford the costumes.

OK. I'll call it the Merry Wives of Bushmills.

Be careful with the title. The Irish writer An MacAodh claims you have plagiarised two of his titles, The Merchant of Ennis and Two Gentlemen of Fintona.

Who'd have thought I'd get a play in Ireland.

Well as I say Will, all the world's a stage.

Give me a quill. All the world's a stage, hmm. I'll be back in six months.

Another De Profundis

The salmon dodges the kingfisher's dive
a corncrake repeats its call for shelter
reality is ebbing from the dying bed
memories drift from Portora shore

Opium
Absinthe
Morphine
  no more

Anointed
last rites
saying
Oscar
we will hear
your voice
cry
again
from a deeper De Profundis
Amen

The ring

Our marriage was two hundred and eighty-five days over, but Zak still wouldn't give back the ring. It wouldn't be two hundred and eighty-six. There had been only one day of happy marriage, my wedding day. There had been too many nights waiting and fearing his return from the Black Bear Inn. The Emergency Room nurse knew I hadn't walked into a door. I had to rid myself of the physical pain and bury the emotional scars. I needed money for freedom and happiness. It was the least I deserved.

One swipe of my Bowie knife and off it came, finger and all. He felt no pain. Marcia saw to that with half a bottle of bourbon down his throat and the other half as an anaesthetic on his finger. I planted the finger upright in his cannabis plant and painted him a message on the back porch. 'Smoke on this'. There was no point taking the finger to Riley the pawn. He wouldn't lend on it.

Me and Marcia rode up on Zak's Harley. He wouldn't be needing it for a while. Riley was about to close up as we walked in. I was in a hurry so I banged the ring down on the counter. 'How much?'

Riley gave it a quick glance. "Fifty bucks."

I knew that was wrong. It had cost me almost five hundred when I'd bought it for Zak. "It's worth more than that. Remember I got it here." I was kinda pleading.

"OK. Fifty-two then."

The increase was an insult and made me mad but not as mad as Marcia. "I think you mean five hundred," she said. Riley laughed and turned his back.

Marcia headed out the door. She was back within thirty seconds.

"You don't understand. Five hundred or I'll blow your balls off and add them to the sign outside." Riley turned to see Marcia pointing a gun at his lower half. He didn't panic but didn't move either. I suspect he never had a woman point a gun at him before, so he was uncertain what to do. Marcia walked right up to the counter. She showed no sign of nerves "Open the till." Even her voice was strong. He didn't reply, just clicked the till open. He put a bundle of notes on the counter. I counted out six hundred and eight dollars. I handed back one hundred and eight. I didn't want Riley thinking me a thief.

I pocketed the five hundred and left him the ring. As we backed out Riley made a grab for something under the counter. Marcia fired. The bullet would have parted his hair if he hadn't been bald. She had been first reserve for the State's Shooting Team.

Marcia was annoyed. She marched Riley to the back of the shop and made him climb into a half full barrel of moonshine. I think it was white lighting. She put the lid back on the barrel, forced it shut but not before punching a hole in the lid. There was breathing space. Marcia wasn't cruel.

We jumped on the Harley and headed for the state line. We saw no police even when we hit Tennessee at eighty. Marcia's grandpa wasn't expecting us but he was accommodating, He appreciated the company. His wife had died three years previous. He still had the loneliness.

Over the next two years we developed a grits business. We dipped them in flavoured moonshine. Blueberry was the favourite. We marketed it as a health product, one of your five a day. We called them Zak Riley's grits with a gold band on the packet and a thumb pointing up. We thought a wedding ring finger might be misunderstood. We sold out to a multi- national four years on and me and Marcia now live in San Francisco.

My cousin came to stay. He told me that Riley had escaped not long after we left. His wife had been worried, wondering why he was late. She had gone to the shop and found him singing in the barrel. She didn't believe a word he said and divorced him. She owns the pawnshop now.

Zak is a bit of a local celebrity. He claimed a black bear had bitten off his finger and swallowed it. He visits local schools to warn kids of the danger of bears and knives.

Me and Marcia have Harleyed Route 66. Twice.

More than essentials

He had abandoned me. My only option was to try to reverse the van back to the crossroads a mile away. Some risk on a road little wider than single track with two-foot deep sheughs on either side.

I never knew why they nicknamed him the Shop Boy. Luigi had been in the same class at school as my grandmother, so he was no boy. He drove the mobile shop that toured the rural roads in the west of the county. The shop element was kind of correct.

He had no Italian blood, was named after a fish and chip shop Luigi's where his mother had worked. I suppose it could have been worse. She had also worked in Barking Malone's, a pet shop. He was over six foot tall, as thin as a rake with a mass of scarlet red hair that wasn't natural but would have worked as a stop signal.

Luigi did have a sense of style even if not age related. He lived in a house up a narrow, grass path about 200 yards from the main road . On rainy days you needed wellingtons to walk it. He had built a small shed at the roadside where he stored his work and his stepping out clothes - well ironed white shirts, a polka dot dicky bow tie, drainpipe trousers, winkle picker shoes and his real pride and joy, a scooter. He cut quite a sight on a summer night, racing through the village at 35 miles an hour, shirt flapping in the wind and skidding to a halt outside Dolan's pub.

In the summer before my last year at school I got a job assisting Luigi in the mobile shop. During the rest of the year he was a solo operator so he wasn't going to miss this opportunity to delegate. He decided that his role for the rest of the summer was to drive, stop, and sit in the cab of the lorry fiddling with a radio he had installed himself. He could only get one station. I didn't mind. I saw myself as a bit of an entrepreneur with Luigi more a chauffeur than leader of the sales operation.

We stocked every essential, from apples to Y fronts, as we toured the farmhouses and isolated cottages often doing forty miles a day. I became an expert on the price of cattle, who had saved hay and turf and sometimes the bringer of sad news about those who were ill or who had died. We got tea at some houses but if we didn't we would pull in and party on brown lemonade, stale crisps and broken biscuits.

The partnership worked well. We had a good summer. Luigi even gave me a few driving lessons. One thing I had noticed was that although most customers came to the back door of the mobile, two or three every week would get into the cab beside Luigi. These customers were mostly middle-aged or older men but there was also a few women. They tended to talk in hushed tones. If there was any danger of being overheard they would head up the road for a short stroll. Occasionally Luigi would take a note from them adding the money to what seemed a sizeable roll of bank notes, a sum that couldn't be earned from operating the mobile.

I used to speculate on the reasons for these personal meetings. I thought perhaps Luigi had the cure for some ailment that tended to effect older people, but I never saw medication of any kind being passed over. I thought perhaps he was hearing confessions. He often had his right hand raised as giving them absolution. Some people regarded him as a half priest in that he had spent two years in the seminary before being expelled for bringing poteen back when he returned from his Christmas holidays. The lecturers in the seminary were gutted as most had paid in advance for their order.

Then on the last Wednesday in August at about eight o'clock my working relationship with Luigi came to an abrupt end. We were stopped at the widow McGrath's our last call of the day. She was always a woman well prepared.. As she was reading her requirements Luigi came round from the cab asking if he could have a word with her. She handed me the list and headed off with Luigi. They had only gone about forty yards when I heard an almighty shout. Mrs McGrath came running back, leapt up into the back of the mobile. She grabbed a pitchfork from our onboard stock of farm implements for sale. Heading straight back towards Luigi shouting

" You cheeky sod. Do you think I'm interested in a dirty drunken eejit like Sean. Tell him to shove his tractor ."

I waited half an hour but there was no sign of Luigi or Mrs McGrath returning. I was told later that she had chased him for nearly two miles. Luigi was last seen doing sixty on his scooter heading to Lisdoonvarna. She never came back to pay for the pitchfork.

Then a bit of luck. McGourty Og who was at least sixty, pulled out of a field a hundred yards ahead on his Massey Ferguson. I waved him down. Well he had to stop. There was no room to pass. I hardly needed to explain the problem. He jumped in the cab, reversed to the nearest gap and with five movements had the van facing back to the crossroads. I offered him a pick from the stock. He took two pairs of Y fronts and a bottle of orange squash.

I did the only thing I could. I turned the key in the ignition and drove off, back to the main road. I took twenty-three packet of crisps and two and a half bottles of lemonade as payment. I decided against a career in retail.

Hazel Siberry

Like a Bird on the Wire,

I have tried, in my way

To be free

A retired GP, Hazel Siberry lives in the beautiful seaside village of Castlerock on the Causeway Coast in Northern Ireland. After retirement she joined a Creative Writing Group just for fun and is enjoying it as a challenge. This is her first publication.

one week in winter

without whisper of warning
blustering easterlies blow

crisp crackling of night frost
sparkling stars Venus low

in the morning no birdsong
still silence of snow

teeth

chattering chil

throw

snowballs in

street

soft slushing of car tyres
as snow turns to sleet

crunchy remnants on pavements
threaten unwary feet

tinkling down drainpipes
thaw is complete

The Ponderosa

Santana anthems loudly thumping
dark Angels glide on petrol power
drugs, booze, tattoos, a history stark
ten shining bikes line up to park
outside the Ponderosa

Charlie Pride's crystal chandeliers lit up
tin sheriff badges, gunslingers kit
silver spurs spangle, with intent looks
they dance the line in cowboy boots
inside the Ponderosa

Angels stroll in, silence speaks invasion
two lines draw up in battle form
tall cowboy hats face helmets down
bottles broken, terse taunts thrown
disturb the Ponderosa

Kiss an angel good morning, Charlie croons
smiles start to spread, tight shoulders slacken
loud laughter now, the joke is clear
a taste of humour, a feast of beer
unites the Ponderosa

LOSS WITH LEONARD

He's gone.... He's gone....

ashen faced   in disbelief   I stand stunned
        bewildered   bereft   broken
my life   my heart   shattered like
        fragile crystal hurled violently against a wall
If only I could wake to find this only a nightmare
        this is real life   I must live it
I am adrift   a sailor after a shipwreck
        wrecked by a storm
I didn't see coming

He's gone....

I grieve   I am alone   I choose to be
        I don't want company
of friends regaling me with platitudes
        things will get better   time will heal
I retreat within myself   I need to live vicariously
        through other people's pain
to feel other people's hurt

He's gone....

I need poetry and song to comfort me
        I know there is no hurt
if first there is not love
        but Oh Love Hurts
sleepless I am haunted by the bittersweet
        words of Miss You Nights
they are the longest

He’s gone....

I sail on   from the shores of love
            past the reefs of grief
to the squalls of hate   now I hate
            him   me   the world
for everything   yet somehow
           hate is healing hurt
despond declining

He’s gone….

Now I know that past that reef
         there is a lighthouse
light feeble and flickering
        getting stronger every day
a crack in the sea wall of despair
       that lets the light in
and with it hope

He's gone….

I am the mute white swan
           who glides serene
paddling feet furious against
         the tide of misery
I am broken but I know
        I can mend

He’s gone….

finally   it’s over
       it’s closing time

He’s gone…………

Not a Fairytale of New York

on our summer vacation my best friend and I
crowded into Manhattan for the Fourth of July
no tickertape welcome big parade or display
just a bargain basement bonanza at Macy's today

after drinks in the Hard Rock we entered Times Square
the pride of American manhood stood there
New York's Naked Cowboy all undressed in white
lustily strumming to rapt crowd's delight

white stetson   tanned torso   hard abs of six pack
guitar at the front   briefest briefs at the back
we stood there entranced by his splendid physique
not to mention his singing or guitar technique

wandering aimlessly onward through laughter and fun
Independence Day crowds just enjoying the sun
stopped short by a vision   both risqué and bold
New York's Naked Cowgirl looked eighty years old

pink stetson and boots   lined face   bleached blonde hair
dugs dangling to waistline   devoid of all care
worse was to come for without shame or fear
she gyrated sideways revealing her rear

pink thong between buttocks   wrinkled crumpled and bare
like old tissue paper   we tried not to stare
slightly stunned we retreated seeking relative calm
to where shih tzu Queen Layla sat enthroned in her pram

such sartorial splendour   red bow in top knot
now New York in summer the pavements are hot
so with haughty indifference Layla proudly displayed
four fine red dog trainers   of a delicate shade

for bizarre entertainment the Big Apple is best
I named but a few   I will spare you the rest
to gawp in amazement or laugh till you cry
please visit Times Square on the Fourth of July

The Mask

The mask was perfect. Sylvia looked intently at her reflection in the harsh light of the Ladies toilet mirror. Her make up had taken a long time tonight but it was worth it, it was perfect. Satisfied, she was now able to enter the bar for this week's Book Club.

As she entered there was a sudden silence. She held her breath, *had they guessed?* At last, a friend, Margot, shouted *Hey Sylvie, we thought you weren't coming, you're late! There's a seat over here beside me.* She felt her shoulders relax and smiled gratefully at Margot as she sat down to discuss last week's book choice. 'Fifty Shades of Grey' had been the much-requested book and this week everyone had read it. The book was discussed with lots of wink-wink moments and hoots of ribald laughter. Someone shouted. *Sylvie, are you going to get John to try that one? "* She smiled a secretive smile and coyly murmured,
Now that would be telling.

At last, it was over, time to go. Margot offered her a lift, but she refused. *No thanks I've got the car with me tonight.* She delayed as long as possible so that she was last to leave. The others had all left the car park by the time she climbed into the seat of her ten-year-old VW Golf. Not the most exciting car in the world but her best friend for the past eight years. *I'm going to miss you old friend,* she mused. Driving slowly out of the village towards the coast, she took care to keep her speed down. She didn't want to attract attention tonight.

At last she reached the small, secluded beach where the group of wild swimmers occasionally met. *No going back now,* she thought as she parked in the darkest corner of the small car park. So far, the plan was going well but now for the hardest part. It had taken years to achieve. Marvelling at her own tenacity, she had nearly given up on several occasions. It had been very hard to be normal, pretending everything was OK despite the reality of coercive control and sexual violence, having to hide the bruises inflicted in alcohol fuelled rages. Thank God for the make-up mask, she had been using it for years.

Thank God too for Sean, a childhood friend from her wild days, long before she met John. He was the only one who knew and understood. Brought up in a strict Presbyterian household, the only child of older parents she had felt suffocated. At age 16 she had run away to London to "live". There a hedonistic drug ridden lifestyle caused her to end up on the street, an addict. Weekly phone calls home painted a very different picture. Sean had saved her, locking her in his bedroom as she endured the torture of cold turkey. When clean she was told of her parents' deaths in a road accident. Sean encouraged her to return home to her old life as a devout churchgoer, living in her childhood home. No-one was ever to know this part of her life.

She had accidentally run into him in Asda, just after he got out of jail. As the respectable wife of a high-ranking police officer, she would never be expected to be in contact with him, a heroin addict, who fed his habit by dealing drugs. A burn phone kept carefully hidden in a hidden compartment of her old Golf allowed them to keep in contact. She had often wondered what that compartment had been used for in the past. Whatever … she had made good use of it.

Sean knew people who knew people, who knew other people. In drug dealing circles there were some very good forgers. There were also experts in money laundering. Nights out as a police wife, forbidden by her husband to drink so that he always had a sober chauffeur, made her party to a lot of sensitive information. After a few drinks a lot of sensitive information was disclosed by other high-ranking officers. She made sure that John could never be marked as the source but that information had paid dividends, not in cash but in kind. Over the course of three years she had managed to obtain another name, taken from a tombstone in Donegal, a girl who died of meningitis aged five. With this name she also obtained a new birth certificate. Thank goodness the birthdate was close to hers. She could still be a Sagittarius -- one less pitfall avoided.

She had always done the Euromillions but never expected it to come up trumps. A substantial win gave her a new Irish passport with a bankroll of her winnings secure in a Euro bank account in her new name. She had made sure Sean had done well out of the deal. He would never reveal her real name, she knew too much about him for that. Anyway in his line, he would be a dead man if he revealed his contacts. She had deliberately told him details of her 'supposed' plan. Even he didn't know her real one.

Stepping out of the car she felt the chill of the night air. At least it wasn't raining. Taking the rucksack from the boot she changed quickly into new, Asda's best, tracksuit and trainers bought with cash on shopping trips and hidden in her Golf. Her high heels and fancy frock were thrown carelessly onto the back seat. Credit card and shopping receipts would not reveal her Asda purchases. The only things she had taken from the house were her swimsuit and wild swimming blanket-coat. Pity she would have to leave coat behind on the beach.

Her next move was vital. She had to remove the make-up mask, carefully putting all the soiled wipes in a bag inside the rucksack. Adding a fetching black wig purchased long ago for her passport photo, no one would recognise her now. She had been dying her hair blonde for years but soon she would revert to her natural colour.

She retrieved her new passport, cards and burn phone from the hidden compartment and prepared to go. The car keys were in the ignition. Her handbag containing her old passport, cards and mobile was left on the seat. The swimming coat was placed on the beach, a real Stonehouse touch. All was ready.

She set off into a very dark November night. The cliff path was rough, but she didn't dare use a torch. It didn't matter, she knew the way. A five-mile walk brought her to the small village where an airport taxi would pick her up at 6am. Booked in her new name there was no need to rush, she had plenty of time.

She felt her spirits lift— everything going to plan. She tried not to think about what she was leaving behind … or about John sprawled in big easy chair, motionless, staring at that interminable Sky Sports channel.

The mask was gone, she was free. By the time they found his body she would be long gone.

Maura Doran

BE HAPPY

Originally from Armagh, Northern Ireland, Maura Doran now spends her time between Derry and Donegal. A former international performing arts examiner with Trinity College London, her work took her into the literary hubs of many overseas countries. She was also an adjudicator for the Hong Kong Speech Festival and lead judge for the Shakespeare Competition, Sri Lanka. When in 2020 world travel was no longer possible, she rekindled her love of writing with the help of a bursary from the Irish Writer's Centre, Dublin. Maura now holds an MA in Creative Writing from the Seamus Heaney Centre, Queen's University, Belfast, Northern Ireland. A member of two Northern Irish Writing Groups, *Words Inc* and *this writing thing* she is also a volunteer story reader for the Verbal Arts Centre, Derry.

OCTOPUS EYES

Mr Smith's wife could talk. She talked so much that silence in her vicinity was impossible. Not only did she talk when she was awake, but she also talked in her sleep. Over the fortythree years of their marriage Mr Smith had learned how to sift through the noise and respond to the important words, the ones that required action – bins, dog, shopping, fix – you get the idea. Sometimes she asked him questions, but she rarely waited for Mr Smith's answers.

So, he had skilled the art of the nod, the frown, the grimace, and other body signals to keep her talking afloat; all without too much effort. He had also honed the ability to turn off whichever ear was closest to her. This was tested when they hired a car in Italy; there he had to drive on the right side of the road. Mr Smith switched ears with the speed of an Olympic sprinter. Mr Smith was very talented indeed.

At the hotel, Mrs Smith talked so much that she didn't hear the Italian waiter explain, in English, that the special of the day was polpi in purgatorio: baby octopus served complete, a local tradition, in a hot chilli sauce. She talked, nodded and ordered the special. Mr Smith tried to dissuade her. She was having none of it, continuing to admire the restaurant décor. Mr Smith ordered the pesce alla puttanesca. The waiter suggested a Sardinian red, Argiolas Costera, luscious and ripe, to accompany the fish dishes. Mr Smith ordered a bottle. The waiter thought how he himself would need a full bottle of Grappa if he had to put up with that constant prattle.

The pesce alla puttanesca arrived first. It was served on a simple white dish. The contrast, a beautiful sight. Crusty bread rested on the side of the plate. Mr Smith bent over to inhale the aroma. This was going to be a special meal. The polpi in purgatorio arrived. Mrs Smith's reaction was somewhat different to his. Oh dear! Poor Mrs Smith when she saw those octopus eyes looking up at her.

For once in her life Mrs Smith was quiet, speechless. Her scream broke the ambiance. The waiter turned back. All was in order. But Mrs Smith complained he should have told her about the eyes. With great decorum the waiter explained that he had indeed mentioned the presentation. Lifting the offending food, he offered another choice. All the while Mr Smith sipped the soft red wine enjoying the subtle flavours of his selection. Mrs Smith told the waiter that she would have one of those, pointing to her husband's fayre. Mood restored, she resumed her chatter. She didn't notice the waiter speak to Mr Smith; something about Mrs Smith, Purgatory, and wine. Mr Smith nodded.

The waiter brought another bottle of Sardinian red to the table.

THE BRIDGE

Large signs flash against the dark sky.

SLOW DOWN

DELAYS ON THE BRIDGE

You brake, slowly.

Your eyes follow the car in front, approaching the bridge you see the left lane ablaze with red brake lights. The right lane is empty. You look around to work out the delay. The tailback stops halfway over the bridge. You sigh. The opposite side a theatre of emergency vehicles, flashing lights, the movements of reflective jacketed emergency crews. A small car, by the bridge railings, is out of place. You glance at the clock: 18.06.

The rain stops. You turn off the wipers. A helicopter sounds above the car. You open the passenger window. A white beam is scanning the river below. You know why. You make a call. It goes to voicemail. You leave a message:

Hi Love, I'll be a bit late. I'm stopped on the bridge. Search and Rescue are out. Someone's jumped. How's the mood today? Feeling any better?

The car in front starts to move. You drive behind it; it turns left. You turn right noticing the time: 18.12.

Following the road, you turn into the empty driveway of a detached two-storey house. The light over the front door is on; the rest is in darkness. She must be running late too. You turn off the car, reach over for your laptop bag. You lock the car, fumble with one hand to find the house key. Opening the front door, you switch on the hall light. A white envelope is propped up on the hall table. Your name is on it. Her writing. A red heart drawn in the right corner. With trepidation you lift the envelope. You have a flashback to the bridge, the out of place car.

The envelope is unopened.

A police car pulls into the drive.

You drop to your knees and howl.

SPILT MILK

Click.

The timer started.

Fifteen minutes to challenge his culinary skills.

George measured the ingredients before tossing them into the blender. Lifting the oven dish to empty in the mix, he noted his error. He hadn't added in the milk. Grabbing the jug, he poured it into the blender. The machine whirred. Milk slopped over the table.

George burst into tears. He wouldn't win the competition.

The judges gave him second place, telling him not to cry over the spilt milk. For a ten-year-old, he was a super little chef.

GOLDEN JOURNEY

Childhood for me was a happy time – despite being the eldest of six and having to be the sensible one. Part of that happiness was spending a lot of time with my two sets of grandparents. My Mum's parents lived in a rural setting in County Tyrone. There we were close to nature, learning how to look after hens, milk the goat and collect berries to make jam. In contrast, Dad's parents lived on a busy road in Belfast. There we listened to Percy French and John McCormack singing from a large brown gramophone. Afterwards we would sing *The Mountains of Mourne* or *Bless this House* at the top of our voices with Granny accompanying us on the piano. Grandad loved to cook, Granny hated cooking – she preferred to sing or write – so the rhythm of the house was well balanced.

For holidays and high days my second sister and I would often stay over with our grandparents in Belfast. Night times we would lie in the big old bed at the top of the house, enjoying the noisy street and the reflecting lights from the constant traffic outside. The bed smelt of lavender, the pillows were deep and soft. Their house was a treasure trove of books, travel souvenirs and pictures. My granny's most precious item was a porcelain vase that she and Grandad had brought back from Italy. The vase took pride of place on top of the piano; vibrant colours depicted nine ladies dancing. My sister and I often pretended to be those beautiful ladies with their elegant gowns and curled golden tresses. We had good imaginations.

One summer night, as my sister and I lay cosy in the big wrought-iron bed, we could hear Grandad humming as he pottered in the kitchen, most likely preparing porridge for the morning. Granny was silent, that meant she was writing. The house was happy, warm, and snug. My sister and I were loved and spoiled as we read our books under thick cotton sheets and a heavy floral bedspread.

Drifting into doziness a loud crash broke the calm. Worried about what might have happened we made our way downstairs towards the noise. Mimi, Granny's black cat, met us on the landing as she scarpered up the stairs. Downstairs the vase lay in three pieces on the floor. The piano looked lonely and incomplete without its usual companion. Granny was upset, complaining about the culprit Mimi. Grandad went in search of a cardboard box into which he carefully gathered up the broken pieces.
Mimi didn't make much of an appearance that night.

Sad to be leaving the next day, my sister and I made a drawing for Granny; we left it on top of the big bed. Our creation couldn't compare with the artisans of Italy, but we hoped that she would enjoy our nine dancing ladies. Summer and autumn came and went, we visited our grandparents many times. Always noting the empty space on the piano and feeling that something was missing.

That Christmas we were excited to be back to stay in Belfast. The house was bright and buzzing with family and friends. All the familiar Christmas signs were in place – the tree, the manger, the cards – and slap bang back in its place on the piano, was the vase. The broken pieces had been put back together and were highlighted with golden dust.

Grandad told us about his Japanese friend who knew how to fix porcelain. He talked about Kintsugi, whatever that was. We listened, but only took in the bit about 'joining with gold'. Anyway, we already knew that he and Granny were joined by their golden rings.

Somehow, the vase was now more than just a travel souvenir; it had become a precious symbol of love, a talking point. It was the star that Christmas.
Later that night, two little girls, tired and happy, flopped into the big bed at the top of the house with Mimi. Their framed drawing of nine dancing ladies looked down on the three of them from the bedroom wall.

My grandparents are now long gone but when I look at the vase I think back to my happy times with them. I also hear my grandad discussing the meaning of Kintsugi. It means 'golden journey'. As an adult I can now fully appreciate its meaning, why the vase commanded so much attention that Christmas.

In Japan, broken items are reassembled and glued together with a precious tree sap and gold dust. No attempt is made to disguise the damage, and the fault lines are beautiful and strong. The powdered gold highlights the fractures, and it becomes part of the object's history.

When we are young, we aspire to perfection in work, appearance, family, and relationships. Dreams are often shattered; life can throw tough blows. We humans are fragile. We can crack. Kintsugi recognises human fragility, that each of us develops our own personal scars as we journey through life. It celebrates our imperfections, which should never be hidden. After all, our cracks could be the birth of something new, just like my grandparents' vase.

Golden Journey was first performed by Gemma Walker-Farren, in the Waterside Theatre Derry, Northern Ireland, as the Ninth Day of Christmas in a Twelve Days of Christmas online performance, December 2020. It was later performed, by Maura Doran herself, at a Tenx9 event in Flowerfield Arts Centre Portstewart, Northern Ireland, May 2023.

olloway

Ruth Holloway

The town of Coleraine in Northern Ireland has been Ruth Holloway's home for over thirty years. She has been writing ever since she was a little girl. A member of two Writing Groups, *Words Inc* run by Libraries NI. and a Zoom writing group, *The Procrastinators,* she prefers to write short stories. Her inspiration comes from horror films, creepy pasta, pangolins and cats. She is drawn to anything strange or mysterious such as Roald Dahl's *Tales of the Unexpected.* Her short story, *The Perfect Wedding Dress* was published in 2022 by Impspired Press. Ruth's ambition is to publish a book of her short stories, but above all, to keep writing.

Dreamy Dave:

The Sudbury Star: Weather warning! Heavy rain predicted for weeks to come.

Friday afternoon 4.15pm

It had rained for weeks. Every day while during the rain, Dreamy Dave had been in detention. He sat there, a wide smile on his face. Mrs Lester looked sternly at him. He should not be smiling in detention. Dave had an incredible imagination, but it frequently got him into trouble. He preferred daydreaming to Maths. He preferred daydreaming to English, History, Science, in fact every subject. He was failing at everything. Dave would have to learn to apply himself which is why he found himself in detention every day. He was content however, because although it was raining outside, in his imagination he was happy, going down a slide, playing in sunshine.

Suddenly the door burst open. Flood water forced its way in, jolting Dreamy Dave into the present moment.

The Sudbury Star: Detention Drama! Dreamy Dave drowns in deluge.

Mr Big

On Tuesday 3rd August, Mr Big waited for the transaction to finish. The drugs were handed over in exchange for a large sum of money.

He always had to be careful to avoid being caught by the police. So he'd arranged for the drugs to be hidden inside pork pies. From a lorry parked outside his men carried many large boxes into his warehouse. The boxes had *Quality Pork Pies* written on their sides.

Once the transaction was completed, he began the painstaking task of retrieving the drugs. He made the younger members of his gang do the dirty work. They were desperate to belong and would do anything he asked of them. They crumbled endless pies into rubbish bins, picking out plastic bags full of drugs from the gooey mess inside.

As he watched them, he sat back and enjoyed a few glasses of the organic wine he'd bought from Tesco's. He was a gangster, but he cared about the environment.

The other gangsters teased him about it. He couldn't bring himself to go vegan though. He loved his cooked ham too much.

The Lion, the Mouse, and the Bird

~ a children's Tale ~

Lion roars, "What a bea-u-ti-ful day!"

Mouse squeaks, "It's cool hanging out with you."

Lion pedals the bicycle. Mouse is balanced on the handlebars.

Bird lands on Lion's cap.

"Can I come along for the ride?" asks Bird.

"Let's go a bit faster," squeaks Mouse.

The three of them whoosh along, the wheels going clickity - click.

Bird panics. "This is too fast for me." He flies off with a squawk.

Mouse exclaims, "Bird pooped on your cap!"

For Lion this ruined an otherwise brilliant outing.

"Isn't it as well you were wearing one," laughs Mouse.

Mouse's chuckle made Lion laugh as well.

The day wasn't a disaster after all.

Obsession

Kirsty was worried about going to the Dentist, but she had a very painful toothache, so she had to go.

When she arrived at Reception, she was asked to take a seat. Directly opposite the seat she chose was a painting of a young peasant girl with blonde plaits and a floral dress.

At first Kirsty didn't pay much attention to the painting until she noticed something strange. The young girl was now holding a dove that wasn't there when Kirsty had first sat down. How did that get there ? At that moment, she was called into the dentist's clinic. She had three fillings, but she was brave. The Dentist said she coped very well.

Before leaving Kirsty checked the painting again. The dove had disappeared, and the young girl was now smiling broadly. As Kirsty left the dentist, she couldn't help but wonder what she had just seen.

The next day, Kirsty made one of her special shopping expeditions. She loved going to charity shops where she always found a bargain. In her favourite shop, after choosing two books and a painting Kirsty was ready to go home. That's when she saw it sitting there. It couldn't be the same painting from the dentist. Yet there it was. It had to be a copy. In this version the girl was now on her own with no sign of a dove. It was priced at £3.99. She decided to buy it.

Back home Kirsty put the painting opposite her bed so that she could keep an eye on it. Maybe these paintings were haunted. But the young girl did not appear sinister. She seemed to be a friendly spirit.

By the following morning, the painting had changed again. The girl was holding a parcel. A box wrapped in red glittery paper. Looking more closely Kirsty was surprised to find that she could lift the box out of the painting. She couldn't wait to open it. Inside it was a tiny carousel. Delighted she wound it up. Miniature horses began to gallop and prance to the music which came from the tiny object. The melody made her head swim, so she lay down on her bed to sleep.

When she woke up, the girl from the painting was standing over her. Kirsty screamed. The girl retreated, climbing into the painting.

Kirsty decided to give the painting back to the charity shop. She was now terrified of it. She doubted the girl meant her any harm, but she was still scared of her.

After she returned the painting, she found she missed it. She wanted it back. She began to think the girl had meant her no harm, so gradually over time she forgot how afraid she had been.

Two months later

Kirsty was in the charity shop when she noticed something familiar. It was the same painting. The price had gone up to £4.99 but she still bought it.

She talked to the painting everyday as if the girl in it was a real friend. But the girl herself never came out of the painting again. However, Kirsty found that she was able to lift out a bracelet which the girl had worn on her arm. Mother of pearl. She put it on her own wrist.

Every day she spent more and more time talking to the painting. In fact, she did little else. The painting slowly took over her life.

Her worried Mum demanded Kirsty give up the painting. Kirsty refused. The next day, while Kirsty was out at another charity shop, her mother took the painting out of her bedroom, and burnt it. That particular painting would do not more harm.

At first, Kirsty was lost without the painting but over time she realised she had to learn to live without it. She regularly checked all the charity shops hoping she would find it, but she never did. She missed it but gradually her life returned to normal.

She was free!

The Child Capsule

A very special task had been assigned to Bob the Robot. During a three year space flight, he had to monitor a sleeping child.

They were heading to planet Nero. Child X12 had been placed in suspended animation for thirty-four months. The Program would wake him up two months before landing so that his body could readjust to normal living. On Earth, the child's parents had given the seven-year-old up for adoption. Planet Nero offered a new, and better, life. As humanoids had evolved differently there than on Earth, its inhabitants were kinder, more intelligent. They had developed knowledge far beyond earthly comprehension. The Program tried to re-locate as many children as possible on Nero.

Bob kept watch day and night because Robots do not need to sleep. Throughout the long flight, he found himself evolving. He was only supposed to monitor Child X12 while he slept, but Bob found that he was experiencing an unusual sensation in his circuitry. He was developing a fondness for the child.

Two months before they were due to land, Bob woke the child as programmed. When Child X12 opened his eyes, they were bright blue. He looked angelic with his blonde curls. He would be easy to rehome.

"Where am I?" asked the child.

"In space. In two months, we will land on Planet Nero."

Child X12 showed no surprise at this. He had other priorities.

"I'm hungry."

Bob opened a packet of cereal. On the spaceship everything was packaged or tinned.

The cereal was bolted down by the hungry boy.

The days passed. Bob and the child played *I-Spy* and *Simon Says*. Child X12 ate a lot of cereal.

Finally, they approached the planet. Landing in a forest, they admired its green and luscious foliage from the windows on the flight deck.

Leaving the ship, they looked for a settlement. Walking down the first road they could find, they met a man cutting down a tree.

"Excuse me," Bob queried, " I'm looking for the Child Re-location Centre."

"You'll be looking for the House of Children in the next valley. Miss Mounty, who runs it, will deal with you."

"Can you take us there?"

"Glad to."

The man led them to his strange-looking vehicle. To the child's delight when it moved off, it did not travel on the ground but flew over the mountain to the next valley.

At the top of the valley, they landed on the front lawn of the House of Children.

"Will you be all right from here?"

"Yes." Bob assured him. "Thank you."

Miss Mounty came out as they approached the front door. She was very tall with glasses and dark curly hair. The child noticed she had mouse ears.

"You're a mouse," he cried.

Miss Mounty laughed. "We all have animal features here."

She turned around to show off her long tail.

"The Program sent us from Earth to find a new home for the child," Bob told her.

"Leave the child with me. I will start the process."

With a pang, Bob realised she meant he should go, should leave the child with her.

"Will the child be happy here?"

"Oh yes," Miss Mounty assured him. "He'll have plenty of company, and we will find him the very best new home."

With an empty feeling, Bob turned to leave. He patted the head of Child X12. He did not want to say goodbye but knew the child was now in good hands. His Mission had been completed.

Going down the steps from the front door of the Home, he wondered how he was going to get back to the spaceship. To his surprise, he found the man had waited on the lawn beside his flying vehicle.

"I thought you had left?"

"Yes I had, but I re-appear when anyone needs me. And you need to get back to the spaceship, don't you?"

"Indeed I do."

"Then let me take you."

As they climbed back into the flying vehicle, for the first time Bob noticed that the man's bare feet had webbed toes.

Back at the spaceship Bob began the three-year journey back to Earth, this time travelling on his own.

Once back on Earth he was given another assignment. Another child in another capsule. A Robot's work is never done.

Kenny Campbell

Originally from Glasgow, Kenny Campbell now lives in Coleraine, Northern Ireland. Originally interested in crime fiction prose this is a medium which he hopes to develop. However, as he is now studying an Open University degree in Arts and Humanities with creative writing, this has enabled Kenny to develop his short story writing skills further as well as opening up other writing genres for him. In 2023 he was awarded a full bursary for the John Hewitt Summer School in Armagh, which was a fantastic opportunity for him to learn from established authors and poets, attend creative writing workshops and network with other creatives. His goals for the future include inspiring others to write, and for his own part, to find time to write more consistently as he is really enjoying the process.

Silenced

Alfred Hastings sped through the streets of Glasgow, the tyres of his new 1951 Mercury 8 click-click-clicking across the cobbled road.

The smell of thick black smoke from the Clydeside factory chimneys he passed filled his lungs, acrid, burned his nostrils, and he coughed painfully. It all flashed him back to the scene he had just left. Gun-smoke replaced factory fumes in his mind. The clicking of the cobbles replaced by the snap-snap-snap of his silenced gun.

***

In the flashback, Alfred saw everything that happened tonight. It played out like a flick book, one image following the one before it in a step-by-step sequence.

He had pulled up in a small, empty backstreet car park. He looked around for anyone that might be about. No one. Click. He stepped out into the relentless rain and started walking towards where he hoped Norman Thompson would be, heading home from his committee meeting. He would be alone, Alfred had been told. Click. There he was, in his long grey raincoat, holding his distinctive red and white umbrella. Alfred approached and said Norman's name, just to be sure, and Norman turned to look at him, no recognition in his eyes. Click.

Before Thomson had a chance to open his mouth Alfred drew his weapon and pointed it at Norman's chest. Snap! Norman stumbled backwards. Snap! A twisted, pained expression on his graying face. SNAP! Thompson slumped to the ground, blood pouring onto the pavement through his jacket, from the wounds on his chest and exit points on his back. It began to run into the gutter. Alfred reached down and checked for a pulse. There was none. Alfred looked at the limp body lying on the pavement before him, feeling numb and without remorse.

Alfred put the gun back inside his jacket, walked the few hundred metres back to his car. He climbed in and started to drive. He didn't know exactly where he was going, but he needed to be anywhere but here.

***

As he looked out of the small windows the cold winter night rain continued to pelt down. Heavy, blurring his vision and trickling down the windscreen like the life that was left before the hangman caught up with him. People were hanged for far less than what he had done recently. Alfred was well aware of that. He had never felt untouchable, but was always careful, discreet, rehearsed, quick. He used a different weapon each time, wore gloves, the process was becoming routine, polished even.

Alfred was no coward, but nevertheless, tonight he started to feel uneasy. Of the five people he had murdered so far, this one had rattled him the most. Norman Thompson was prominent in the local community. He had a wife, three school age children. Alfred had gunned him down on his way home from his company committee meeting not quite half an hour ago.

The guilt began to pang at him like the large scar on his left arm from knife fights of his youth, running with the razor gang from his street. He scratched the scar idly, remembering again how it always throbbed after a night like this. He drove down to a secluded spot and slowed to a stop. Getting out of the car, Alfred looked around him. No one there. He walked over to the handrail on the riverside. He planned to throw the weapon into the dark waters. Then the guilt would surely diminish again.

He closed his eyes for a moment. The haunting images and sounds returned strongly. Not just from tonight, but from all the nights. Eyes open. Images still there. Alfred screamed out, banging the gun on the handrail as he did so. The rain sloshed down his brown leather jacket. It mixed with the sweat on his distressed face, mixed with the tears which formed in his eyes. Drips that fell from the gun turned into drops of blood in Alfred's mind's eye. With every drip, Hastings started to feel like he wanted to follow them on their steady journey into the river. Overwhelmed, he started to climb the handrail intending to jump into the river.

He closed his eyes again, trying to block out what he had done tonight. But the images in his mind grew stronger once more. Pictures swirled around, becoming clearer as they went. He went back through the flick-book memories. Click, click, click, snap! Thompson's grey dying face before him. There was no look of judgement, no anger, simply acceptance that his secret sins had caught up with him.

Alfred began to climb back down, more out of curiosity than release. He wanted to know if there was any way he could have stopped himself tonight.

He slumped on the ground, back against the barrier,

pondered his life as the dark sky mirrored his overcast demeanour. He thought of all the things he had done over the years, the acts of anger, aggression, needless violence, the path his life had journeyed. It had all led to the cold-blooded murder of five men. None of them innocent men, but they didn't deserve to die.

Alfred sat there for a few minutes, the rain coming down in sheets now. There were flashes in the sky, loud rumblings, but no flashbulb memories now. There was a press-gang snapping shots of Thomson at the other end of town, no doubt, but to Hastings, the sounds and flashes became just another storm passing over.

Alfred regained his composure and stood up, tossed the gun over his shoulder into the Clyde. The splash sounded to him like closure, freedom almost. Maybe the hangman wouldn't get him just yet. With that he walked back to his car and climbed in. He was just glad to get out of the rain.

You are safe here.

Dad will be home soon from work. Pat was worried again as he looked out of his window. *What will he say to me, what will he do? Maybe I could explain? I don't even like cigarettes; it was just to show off to my mates. He will be so disappointed.* A voice from across the room brought him back from his thoughts.

'Hello, Pat.'

Pat turned from the window, his expression remained uneasy and without any recognition in his eyes. *Who is this guy? Why is he here? Can't he see I'm busy?*

'What are you looking at, Pat? Anything interesting?' asked John, Pat's Carer.

'Emm... well, I'm not sure actually,' said Pat with a slight chuckle.

'That's OK Pat. I don't think much is happening either. Shall we go for a coffee?'

'Who are? Do I know? You?' *Why is he asking me if I want coffee?*

'I'm John, your friend. We often have coffee together. I'd like to go to the café with you, Pat. Would you like to join me sir?

'Well... OK, I guess', replied Pat with reluctance.

'This way, sir.' Motioning to the door and taking Pat's hand, John gently led the way down the hall to the café, with Pat walking beside him. Pat sat in his favourite chair by the window, looking out to the garden. John made a decaf cappuccino with frothed milk and chocolate sprinkles, and set it on the table before Pat.

'What's this?'

'Cappuccino, it's your favourite,' said John with a smile.

'It is? How did you know?'

'Just a lucky guess I suppose!' quipped John.

Pat accepted this, and started drinking his coffee with loud slurps. He looked very happy with life.

The pair sat there, chatting about the activities of the evening in short, disjointed sentences. Pat expressed an interest in going to the cinema room later with his wife Jackie. He said the other day about his new shoes and is now wondering if someone could help him polish them. John told him that this would be no problem. Pat looked very relaxed as if he would really enjoy his date night with Jackie.

Back in room four, John helped Pat out of his blue slippers and took the new black shoes out of their box from Pat's wardrobe. The polish was in the top drawer. With a little help Pat shined his new shoes, enjoying the smell. He liked the way the shoes looked so smart when he was finished. It reminded him of his youth, going to dances with Jackie.

Between the two of them they slipped them onto his feet and put on a freshly laundered blue striped shirt. Pat looked at himself in the mirror door of his wardrobe. He saw himself as he was back then: young, fresh faced, handsome, smiling. He wondered if Jackie was getting dressed up too.

Jackie arrived around eight, dressed in the outfit that she used to wear before Pat started becoming unwell. She met Pat outside his room. They looked fondly at each other before slowly walking hand in hand to the cinema room. There was a large box of sweet and salted popcorn and two large cups of cola waiting for them at the seats. They both looked very happy as John put an old film on. They started settling down to watch the movie together. Before John headed on to chat to some of the other people in Bluebell House, Pat looked over at him, and his eyes seemed to say, 'thank you.' John smiled and mouthed 'you are welcome' in response.

The next evening, Pat stood at his window again, looking out for his Dad. He looked at his watch, seven-thirty. *Dad must be nearly home.* He thought anxiously. Every evening Pat would begin getting restless soon after dinner. He would glance around, before wandering along to his room. By the window is where he liked to stand. Pulling the curtains open just enough to be able to peek outside, his eyes would scan the street below. Looking out for his Dad, who was a traditional, Brethren sort of man. He wouldn't be impressed with the whole situation.

He knows I'm here. He knows about the cigarettes I stole yesterday. He must do. What will he say?

'Hello, Pat…' It was Jackie this time; she had come in a little earlier than usual to surprise him. Pat turned from the window, and smiled broadly, distracted from his worry. Jackie was holding a helium balloon and had a bottle of wine in her other hand.

'Happy anniversary, dear.' She said.

'Is it?'

'Yes darling. Sixty years ago today we were in St. Andrews. Do you remember?'

'How could I forget that? Was it so long ago? It feels like yesterday.'

Jackie embraced her husband and held him for a long moment. 'Let's get you dressed in your suit Pat. I have a surprise for you.'

The whole family had gathered upstairs in the dining room, which was decorated with many photos from over the last sixty years. As Pat and Jackie entered the room later in that evening, there were cheers and a round of applause.

Zenith

A knock at the door, the distinctive tap-tap, tap-tap, tap-tap-tap she always used to let him know it was her.

'Who's there?' George Anderson called out with caution as he habitually did, just to be sure.

'It's Selena, Grandpa, let me in, it's freezing out here!'

George's anxiety eased a little as he lifted himself out of his chair, crossing his living room leaning on his walking stick as he went. Unbolting the four locks on his front door, a flurry of snow blew in when it opened. Selena hurried inside. George checked no one else was around, bolting the door again behind them.

'You've not got the fire on Grandpa, you must be freezing! Here, I'll get it lit if you go and make us a hot drink.'

'I have warm clothes on Selena, it's too expensive to put that thing on.'

'Oh, don't be daft, you'll catch your death in here!'

After leaving a bag of groceries in the kitchen, Selena started a fire, Her hair was the colour of the fresh flames.

A few minutes later George appeared from the kitchen with two steaming mugs of the only hot chocolate he had left in his cupboard. It tasted horrible, but it was hot, and with a few teaspoons of sugar it was bearable.

As the room heated, the coal glowed and sticks crackled on the hearth, sooty wisps swirled through the room. The pair began chatting, catching up on the news since Selena had last visited about a week ago. After a while she asked her go-to question:

'Tell me again about the ocean Grandpa, what is it like?'

George smiled a gentle smile, though still had a lifetime of sadness in his eyes. He glanced around the small, dim room, as he thought back to those days.

'It's special, Selena.' His eyes came alive.

'It's like the lake in town, but it goes on forever, azure blue to beyond the horizon. There's no border guards so no one stops you. It feels like freedom. It used to be like that everywhere. The country of Zenith used to be so beautiful.'

George stopped, overwhelmed with emotion, fighting to hold back nostalgic tears.

'No one I know has been there since I was a boy, 'he said, his head lowered.

'Why is that?'

'When I was about ten, things changed. Dangerous people were voted into the Assembly. They brought in stricter and stricter policies to inhibit our freedom in Zenith. People were forced to move to this appalling city of Zenith Central. All sorts of restrictions became normal. But you know this Selena, so why do you bother me with such questions?'

The pair sat in awkward quiet. Beside the open fire, Selena still felt a chill in her bones. She wanted to know more, but understood her grandfather struggled to talk about such things. He was one of very few people who had lived through all of it, and survived. He had witnessed the decline of ordinary peoples lives into the confined existence which was now the norm in Zenith Central. He had experienced all kinds of horrors. She didn't want to push him too much on the subject, painful as it was for him.

~ ~ ~ ~ ~

As his only surviving family member, Selena visited her Grandfather every week. As this winter continued, he started to decline. His eyesight was fading. His mood was often lower than usual. Selena became more and more worried about him. One day when she visited, George looked very frail indeed.

'Selena' he wheezed, as they sat beside each other on his faded sofa.

'I need to tell you something, something very important.'

'What is it Grandpa?'

'You must leave Zenith Central!'

'What?' Her forehead creased. 'But that's impossible! How would I even...?

'I don't have long left in this world Selena, but you

have your whole future ahead of you. Don't waste it here in this dreadful city. You deserve a life free from restriction, where you can pursue dreams, explore the world, find your place. You have potential way beyond what can be realised within these city walls. Don't you realise you can do anything?'

George stared into her eyes, urging her to listen, grasp what he was saying.

As she took hold of her Grandfather's skeletal hand, looking back at him, she tried to process what he was saying. For a brief moment she wondered if he was becoming mentally confused. Then, once the initial shock started to subside:

'But I'm so young. I don't feel I could...'

'Your youth is what you need to be able to do this Selena. Your parents didn't live to see you blossom. I see who've become. You don't need to change your life overnight. Just get to the coast, and see what you …and this country of Zenith… could be like. You must do this!'

Tears formed in her eyes as she realised how much he meant what he was saying. Taking a deep breath, she asked:

'What do you want me to do Grandpa?'

~ ~ ~ ~ ~

George's funeral was a small bleak affair. Only a handful of people attended in keeping with the restrictions on public gatherings. Selena, his only family member, thanked his neighbours for attending. Her friend Nathan was there too. Seeing her grief, he hugged her. As he did Selena whispered in his ear:

'Meet me tonight at eleven p.m. at the corner of Bishop's Lane and Institution Row. Don't tell anyone, come alone.'

She kissed his cheek and walked away. Although Nathan trusted her, he was alarmed by the secrecy surrounding her suggestion.

The Enforcers assigned to supervise the funeral began to hurry any remaining mourners away from the grave shouting at Nathan to move it along. He looked at the way Selena had gone, back towards her flat at the other end of town, as the snow melted quickly in the late March sun.

~ ~ ~ ~ ~

By the time Nathan reached Bishop's lane that evening, Selena was already there. Showing signs of extreme nervousness, she asked Nathan if he was sure he hadn't been followed. He was sure.

'What's going on Selena?'

'This goes no further Nathan, you tell no one, OK?'

A brief pause, a deep intake of breath.

'Okay, what's the story?'

Selena picked up a large stone. With as much stealth as possible, she struck the fourth brick from the left on the second row of the low wall at the side of the lane, as her Grandfather had instructed. After a couple of blows, the brick came away. Lifting out a small package from behind it, Selena then replaced the brick, kicking away any small bits of stone which had fallen to the floor.

'I'm not sure I want to know what that is, Selena, but we need to get away from here!'

With the package stuffed under Selena's jacket, they walked a few hundred metres back to her apartment, at speed but not so fast as to draw attention.

Once safe at home, Selena ushered Nathan in, locking the front door and closing the curtains.

'You need to get me up to speed here Selena, what the hell is going on?'

'Clear those books off the table. Let's look at what's in this. Grandpa said we would need it.'

When she unwrapped the package on the dining table they gasped in unison at its contents, an old paper map on thick, quality paper. They spread it out on the table. The smell of old parchment wafted through the room.

Nathan unfolded the page to full size, dumbstruck for a moment.

'This is a map of the original country of Zenith. I think Grandpa must have had it from years ago.'

'Why did he want us to have it, Selena? What story did he tell you?'

'He said we would need this to....'

'Stop right there Selena. Whatever the heck this is about, I'm out. They will string us up for this! Look at this! It shows all the areas around Zenith Central, all the way out to the sea. No, no, no. This is really dangerous.' He began to stride around the room, head spinning. Yet he did not leave.

As he paced Selena explained everything George had told her. That there was a beautiful world out there beyond the city limits, that he wanted them to go there, that they must.

'If they find you with this, you know what they'll do to you! And I'm involved now too. Shit! I know we were hoping to try to visit a different part of the Zenith countryside over Spring Equinox, but come on!? We can't just abandon our entire lives here in the city.'

Nathan wasn't as convinced as she hoped he would be about this. Maybe it would just take him a little longer for him to process it all. She folded the map again, packed it away.

She waited as he paced , deep in thought. She watched him calm down gradually. At last, he sat down.

'What?' Nathan asked sheepishly.

'So you're in, then?'

~ ~ ~ ~ ~

On the day of the Spring Equinox each year a large festival was held in the City Centre to celebrate the founding of the modern Zenith State. Everyone was there. All the

Enforcers were on duty, supervising this rarely permitted gathering of citizens. Enjoying loud music and revelry, everyone gathered together in a large crowd.

Selena and Nathan knew this was their chance. With all they wanted to take with them from their old lives packed into rucksacks on their backs, they wandered around the fringes of the City Centre, looking for an opportunity to escape.

A few of the official vehicles which the Enforcers drove were parked unoccupied around the sides of the main squares.

'Here, you check these on this side. I'll check the rest, maybe one still has a key in it.'

'You sure about this? If we get caught...' protested Nathan.

'We'll only get caught if you don't hurry up!'

They both checked the first few cars. They were all locked.

'Now what?' exclaimed Nathan.

Selena spotted another parked further away down a side street. Within a minute, she had the door unlocked. As fortune would have it, the keys were in the ignition.

'No one will notice us in this. It's normal to see Enforcers' cars driving round town. Come on, jump in, I'll drive. Do you trust me, Nathan?'

'I wouldn't be here if I didn't. But this is madness.'

His nerves on edge Nathan looked around him. Completely unsure of this, he climbed into the passenger side anyway, slouching down in his seat, the tinted windows hiding him. Selena took a moment to adjust the mirrors, put on her seatbelt. Starting up, she pulled off in low gear, turning towards the fringes of the city.

They relaxed a little as they drove towards the outer sectors of Zenith Central. Few people were around. As they had hoped, nearly everyone was celebrating, including the Enforcers it seemed. Approaching the city limits, they found a chain-link gate in the border wall. However, on reaching it they saw two Enforcers guarding it, turning towards their approaching car, revealing that they were armed with rifles as they did so.

Selena floored the accelerator, speeding right at the gate sending the guards scrambling out of the way. The gate flew open. A flurry of bullets ricocheted off the back of the bullet-proof vehicle. Selena cried out, the sound a mixture of fear and excitement. Nathan allowed himself a whoop as well. Adrenalin pulsed through both of them, their bodies in a state of fight or flight.

'We are really doing this!' exclaimed Nathan, looking over his shoulder, seeing no one giving chase.

They were on their way out of Zenith Central for the first time in their young lives. Nathan looked at the map.

> 'After about a hundred miles, the highway breaks up into smaller roads. We take any of them going east, after we pass a place called Hope farm.

~ ~ ~ ~ ~

Several hours after crashing through the city gates, using up the very last of their fuel, Selena and Nathan parked beside a deserted coastal bay. They sat there for a minute, drinking in the view of spring sunshine glistening on a clear azure ocean. Then looking at each other with excitement, they realised how eager they were to get into the water. As they climbed out of the car, Nathan smiled at Selena with undiluted joy.

'Just between us, in future we'll call this place New Dawn beach.'

'I love that! Now how about a swim? I'll race you to the water!' Selena discarded her outer clothes, threw off her shoes and socks.

'Hey, wait up!' whooped Nathan, wrestling his arms out of his jumper, leaving it with his jeans on the white sand. The practicalities of their future could be discussed later. The water was calling them now.

Ian Garner

An invitation to join the Morden and District (M.A.D.) Writers' Circle in Cambridgeshire, England, in the mid-1990s sparked Ian's interest in Creative Writing. On moving to Northern Ireland in 2001, Ian continued to develop his fiction writing while pursuing a scientific and business career. On his retirement in 2022 he joined the Creative Writing group, Words Inc, based in Coleraine, Northern Ireland. The pieces in this Anthology will be his first published fiction, and a step on from the occasional short story contribution, as a M.A.D writer, to local parish magazines.

Footnotes:- 1.An Abecedarian piece of writing is one in which the first letter of each successive line of writing follows in alphabetical sequence.

2. The final line is adapted from Wannabe, The Spice Girls

Two x two ≠ 4

After their double wedding, the newlyweds pose for a photo. The brides are chatting.

Alfie says I'm simply perfect.
Beautiful, my Jim calls me.
Charmers, both.
Decidedly delicious.
Engaging as well.
Forget the engagement, we just headed right down the aisle.
"Grooms for hire." Fancy that.
"Have a pretend Happy (two-day) Marriage" the ad said.
It's "In the bag" it said.
"Jollies all weekend" – or was it, "A jolly weekend"?
Know what I think? And keep this to yourself.
Let's hear it then.
Matrimony seems fun.
Nuptials now, but will we want divorces by Sunday?
Oh, you cynic.
Propose to him for real, I dare you!
Quiet! Alfie might run for the hills.
Ready for the reception?
Sure. It's gonna be a blast!
"Totes"!
"Unions-R-Us" – unless something goes wrong.
Very unlikely – the vows were optional.
Well, they said "wedded bliss guaranteed".
"X-rated honeymoons" too!
Yowzer!
Zig-a-Zig, Ah.

A bouncy castle, ventriloquist's dummy, and Russian tank

~ after *The Lost Lost Property Office* by *Roger McGough* using three random items given as a stimulus ~

Teddy stared down at the vodka in his glass. Booze had become his life raft, keeping him just out of reach of the abyss waiting to draw his fast-fading career into its unseen depths. Once a popular act in end-of-pier summer shows, his ventriloquism act, "Teddy Thompson and Charlie Chuckles", had fallen victim to waning demand. Booking agents had stopped calling when he could no longer feign immobile lips while his dummy, Charlie, spoke. Worse his alcoholic tremor now made the dummy quake as if in fear.

'I've still got a few more shows in me, Charlie. Even in this second-rate travelling circus.'

In the mirror, staring back at him, thinning hair atop gaunt features, a frayed shirt collar and grey bowtie, told a different story. Breathing in, he paused as if to sigh, then a faint, disembodied voice uttered,

> 'Cull the other one, Teddy. I can't even talk crocker any more.'

From an open case on the floor beside him, the prone figure of Charlie stared back at him, a rictus grin framed by shiny black hair, bright green eyes, and dimpled cheeks. Unlike his co-star, Charlie sported a dapper black dinner suit, and shiny black shoes with white spats. As his long-time companion, Charlie gave voice to Teddy's inner dialogue.

'Thanks, Charlie. Don't hold back.'

A circus hand shouted at the door of his tiny caravan.

'Five minutes, Teddy. The boss says to keep it clean, it's the kids' matinee show.'

'Hear that, Charlie?'

'Yes. I must not swear at the little goys and girls, gless their little cotton socks.'

'Or we'll both be for the chop, and you'll become firewood.'

Teddy pulled a white cotton glove onto his left hand then, leaning towards the case, he slid his gloveless hand under the dummy's back to find its controls and, lifting him out of the box, Teddy rotated Charlie's head to face him.

'I hope you warmed your hand.'

'Always for you, Charlie.'

With the dummy secured, Teddy drew the curtain covering the rectangular caravan window. He squinted as the afternoon sun poured in, lighting just his eyes and forehead.

'It's just like looking out of the driver's hatch in the tank I drove on my national service.'

'Not the tank again.'

'Steady, Charlie. I do the sarcasm.'

Sounds of commotion outside caught Teddy's attention. Eyes now adjusted to the brightness, he saw Binky the Russian circus clown in full dress and greasepaint shouting, waving his arms and propelling his large bulky frame across the showground towards a group of boys gathered by the bouncy castle, which seemed to be sagging. Teddy saw the boys' knives glint in the sunlight as they slashed and stabbed the castle. Comical as the sight of Binky running was, his clown's blue curly wig bouncing up and down and the wide waist hoop of his over-sized yellow and black checked trousers swinging from side to side, Teddy saw fresh danger.

'Mind that pile of elephant droppings, Binky,' Teddy muttered, 'Ooh, too late.'

Binky's flopping clown shoes caught on the dung, and, as if in slow motion, his arms wheeled as he became momentarily airborne. Mouth agape, he belly-flopped and slid along the rain-soaked field, his red-nosed face buried in the mire. Onlookers applauded the impromptu slapstick and the boys paused to turn and jeer at Binky's misfortune before disappearing into the crowd. Teddy watched on, a faint smile on his lips.

'You should put that in your act, Binky, old son.'

Groaning, winded, Binky rolled onto his back. Mud-blackened with makeup smeared across his cheek he stared skyward only to see the now flaccid grey castle turrets falling towards him.

'Ginky's in trouble,' Charlie said, 'we should rescue our Russian conrade.'

'Comrade Binky?'

'Yes. This room can be your tank. Take it onto the battlefield.'

'A Russian tank to save the Russian clown who is hors de combat.'

Teddy felt inspired.

'Charlie, you be Gunner Gregor and I'll be tank Commander Chekov.'

Teddy held the dummy as if to attention.

'Gunner Gregor recorting for duty, Connander Chekov, sir.'

'To save Binky we've got to clear a path. The Winnebago over there, let's tear it wide open.'

'The circus chief's trailer? It's not in the way.'

'I know, but I'll feel better. Call it revenge for losing our contract. Ready, Gunner?'

'What is the garing, Connander?'

'The bearing?'

'Yes, sir. The garing. I need to coint our gun.'

'Bearing is dead ahead, twenty yards.'

Chekov heard cries from the battleground reverberating inside the tank. He saw Binky's feet kick wildly as the heavy bouncy castle fabric fell, smothering the clown's body.

'Gun ready.' Gregor yelled.

'Steady. Wait for it... Fire,' Chekov commanded.

In great excitement, Gregor declared,

'Firing. Let's glast that trailer to dust. Gurst it and gatter it.'

'Yes, burst it and batter it. Avenge Comrade Binky.'

'Trailer destroyed, sir, but I fear Ginky is lost.'

Battle weary, but elated, Chekov raised his vodka glass in salute,

'Cheers, Binky. Valiant to the end.'

Teddy opened his caravan door; he breathed in the sweet smell of victory. A group of circus hands ran towards the collapsed castle, and while they struggled to lift the heavy fabric off the now still Binky, Teddy adjusted his bowtie and stepped out onto the show ground.

'One more time, Charlie?'

The dummy's head swivelled to look at Teddy,

'Yes sir, greak a leg, Connander Chekov.

'We really must do something about your Bs and Ps, Charlie.'

'You getcha,' Charlie replied.

Predator-Prey

~ One situation. Two viewpoints. Separate voices ~

You stepped out for a moment, so I seized my chance.

I'd just stepped out. You seized your chance.

Handbag on the chair back.

It was hot. I'd opened the window.

Open window, sun blind gloom. I was in.

You were in fast.

Someone coming back. Doppler heel clicks, getting louder, closer.

I'd left the door open. It's now closed.

You open the door. I am gone.

Window blind swaying. No breeze.

Such an easy target, phones.

My phone is not in my bag.

You never knew.

I knew you'd been.

Murder They Wrote – Penultimate section.

A murder mystery composed in sequence by six authors in six sections.

Lodd yawned as he put his coffee cup back onto his desk. Early starts on a Monday were always a challenge, more so when leading a murder investigation. His late Sunday spent at Huntley Hall interviewing suspects did not reveal anything, but he was sure he would find evidence that would reveal which of the siblings had murdered Charles.

'I can feel it in my water,' Lodd thought. 'Maybe more than one of the blighters did it. We need to check their alibis. And as for Mrs Grimsden, her loyalty to this strange family was overly protective.'

The ping of an incoming text brought him back to the present and on reading, he smiled, thinking,

'This will stir things up.'

Sitting back in his chair he stretched, arms upwards, mouth opening wide to release another yawn as Kate Willis entered his office.

'Late night?'

She dropped a manila folder labelled "Pathologist" onto his desk, just missing his coffee cup.

'Late night, sir,' Lodd countered.

'Sir.'

Detective Sergeant, Kate Willis was a thorn in Lodd's side. Easily the brightest of the recent intake of fast-track graduates to his team, her sharp wits and energy often left him trailing in her wake, and she knew this. Lodd regained his composure. Sitting forward at his desk he glanced toward the folder and then to Kate.

'Charles Shrike was drugged with ketamine,' she said.

Opening the folder, he glanced at the report. Kate continued,

'It was in the milk glass at the bedside and in his stomach. Only enough to cause light sedation.'

'Suggesting he could have been aware of the attack and been powerless to resist?'

'Yes, sir, the blood spatter over the walls and ceiling confirmed Shrike's heart was beating hard when he had his throat cut.'

'Poor bastard.'

'The nature of the wound suggested the killer knew how to handle a knife.'

'Check the alibis we got for the brothers, Henry and John.'

'So, you still think one of them is likely to be, as you put it, sir, a "knife-wielding psycho"?'

'Tell me about it.'

'What about Marisa?'

He stifled another yawn, 'Ketamine. That's used on horses, isn't it? Powerful stuff. Marisa is the horsey one. Check her alibi too and see if she's pally with any bent vets.'

As she nodded Lodd tossed the report aside, planted his hands onto the edge of the desk and in one swift movement pushed himself and his chair away from the desk and stood up. Lifting his coffee cup, he took a long swig. She suppressed a grin as he spat the coffee back into the cup, coughed, swore, wiped his mouth on his jacket sleeve, and said,

'Stone cold. Come on, Willis. With me.'

Lodd tossed her his car keys, intending to wrong-foot Kate. Without missing a beat, she caught the keys, and said.

'No morning briefing?'

'Sergeant Brand's got that. We've new evidence and we're off to see Arthur Shrike's solicitor, old Mr Thornton.'

Denying Kate further detail, he headed towards the exit door. She gathered her note pad and bag hurrying behind him.

'Keep up Sergeant,' Lodd said, shouting to ensure his C.I.D. team could hear.

Lodd dropped into the passenger seat and, as he

pulled the car door closed, he looked across to Kate. She was unhappy at not being fully informed of events and returned the glance, scowling. Unphased he again yawned. Before she could look away, Lodd's gaping mouth gifted her the sight of his furred tongue and delivered a pulse of coffee breath. She knew that at least two of her senses were working. Suppressing any sign of disgust, denying Lodd a reward for his behaviour, she started the car and moved off.

He continued,

'There is another Will.'

'That's the new evidence?'

'Just got a text from the Met boys, email to follow. The Will was at Charles' London home. It's more recent than the one read out last week by Thornton.'

'Have you seen the email?'

'Sir.'

'Sir.'

'Give me a chance. It's in my Inbox now.'

Lodd relayed a summary of the message,

'The Will found was drafted for Arthur Shrike by Thornton two months before he died In this newer version John gets the Hall and the paintings, Marisa, the horses and the other brothers a pittance.'

'Then Arthur Shrike knew his son wasn't missing in

action, kept this quiet and changed his Will in John's favour?'

'Bright girl. In his Will, Shrike described John as his "lost, and now returned, beloved son." The Met also found emails to Charles from a U.S.- based security consultant sent two months ago.'

'About John?'

'Yes. He must have had his suspicions about John's disappearance. Something Mrs Grimsden said last night now makes sense. The old girl said that on one of Charles' rare visits to see his father she overheard Arthur telling Charles to "mind his own business about who he chooses to leave his money to". She also said John was always Arthur's blue-eyed boy and that she was the only one who knew he would be returning home in time to hear the Will.'

'And then he learns that John was alive and still in South America and could be favoured in a new Will. That's motive enough to try to suppress the latest.'

'Now you see why I want to talk to Thornton.'

As she parked at the solicitors, Kate saw that the car bay with Thornton's name plate was unoccupied.

'Looks like he's out.'

Lodd had already left the car, and she heard the urgency in his voice just before he slammed the door shut.

'Bloody hell, he may have been tipped off. Come on.'

She followed him as he hurried into the Solicitor's

office, his broad Yorkshire accent booming.

'Police. Is Mr Thornton in?'

Kate saw Lodd moving towards the door bearing Thornton's name.

'You can't just go in,' the receptionist said.

Ignoring her plea, Lodd rammed his shoulder firmly to the door as he pushed down the door lever. The door stayed shut. Lodd rebounded in surprise.

Kate smirked, and the receptionist finished her sentence,

'It's locked. Mr Thornton is off sick today.'

Lodd was distracted by his jarred shoulder, so Kate said,

'Was he well last Friday?'

'Oh, yes. Fit as a fiddle, I'd say.'

'Did he make the call?'

'No, it was his housekeeper, Helen Grimsden.'

Lodd and Willis looked at each other.

'Have you ever met her?' Lodd said.

'No. Mr Thornton has never mentioned her.'

'We know his home address, thanks. Willis, you

drive, and I'll radio ahead to see if we can get a patrol car for back up.'

'Expecting trouble?'

'Something's up.'

Lodd finished his radio calls as his phone notification alert pinged.

'Another email from the Met.'

He updated Kate,

'Helen Grimsden witnessed the latest Will. They also found a handwritten note from her to Charles attached to his copy.'

'Surely she's related to Mrs Grimsden?'

'We need to find out. She's a common thread in all this.'

'I'll ask forensics to compare DNA from the note to Charles with our suspects' DNA.'

'Add Helen to the suspects list. I'll want to speak to her.'

'But what is the link to her and Charles?'

'Maybe old Arthur Shrike got his leg over with Mrs Grimsden years back, and Helen is his daughter.'

'And the children's half-sister.'

'Maybe that's why Mrs Grimsden feels so bound to the family.'

'Maybe,' Kate stressed the word, mocking Lodd's pet prefix, 'Charles won't be the only one to die.'

'Good point, Sergeant. Hold that thought.'

Kate was concerned about Lodd's and his flights of fancy, thinking,

'He's off in his own world. His theories could have come from the imagination of an amateur writer of crime fiction.'

'We need to get some evidence, sir.'

The car radio squawked.

'P.C. 247 to Control. Shots fired. Officer down. Thornton's house.'

Police Control replied, 'Received 247. Ambulance and armed response vehicle now en route.'

'247. That's Sean Hackett,' Lodd said and took the radio handset, 'D.I. Lodd here. What's happened, Sean?'

'When we got to the house, sir, we saw a body face-down just across the front threshold. Male. Looked like he was trying to get away, was shot in the back at close range. Quite a mess.'

'Thornton?'

'We tried to get closer using cover, but we were spotted, and someone fired both barrels at us from an upstairs window. Tree branches took most of the shot, but Jim, PC Todd, was hit in the leg.'

'Is the gunman still in the house?'

'I don't think so. While I was getting Jim to cover, I heard a car engine start and a green open-topped sports car sped down the drive, exiting onto the road, heading north. Two people on board. One male, one female. The female was driving. A redhead.'

'Lodd to Control. Get an all-points call out for that car, reported heading north.'

Turning to Kate, he added, 'Marisa's a redhead.'

'And Huntley Hall's due north.'

'Then that's where we're going. "Blues and Twos", Sergeant. Step on it.'

'Yes, sir,' she said. 'Agatha Christie does Gothic horror,' she thought.

Mary Farrell

From 2019-2023 a Facilitator of Pen and Paper, a u3a Writers Group, in 2024 for The Library Authority in Northern Ireland, Mary Farrell facilitates Words Inc, the Coleraine Library Creative Writing Group, and also co-ordinates another independent weekly Writing Group called Sanderlings in Portstewart, a local seaside town. On Zoom each week she runs a Creative Writing Group for AsIam, an Irish charity which works with autistic adults.

She has been a member of CIEP, The Chartered Institute of Editing and Proofreading, UK, and is in her second year as a member of the Judging Panel for the Weekly Prompts Competition run by the Reedsy Online Publishing Company. She is also the Consultant Creative Writing Facilitator for Impspired Press, based in Lincoln.

Her first Collection of her trilogy of varied pieces, *It's like Walking a Tightrope* was published in September 2021, the second *Out of the Chrysalis* in May 2022 and the third, *A Phoenix Still Rising* in May 2023. *Springboards: a Creative Writing Manual for Beginners through to Facilitators,* and *The Kingdom,* her debut Collection of short stories, the first part of *The Circle Trilogy,* were both published in October 2022. The second part of the Trilogy, *Maybury,* was published in November 2023, and the last segment, *New Asgarth,* will be launched in October 2024, as part of the annual Swell Festival in Portrush, Northern Ireland. She is the Editor of the first two Anthologies in the North Coast Writers Trilogy, *Irish Hares and Seahorses,* 2022, and *Spun Yarns and Woven Words,* 2023, also published by Impspired Press .

A First of January Tale

Quill poised between his lean fingers, brow furrowed, Mr B Ignatius Wolf, BA (Drama), PhD (Forensic Science) scowled at the blank page in front of him. Not a disciple of self-restraint, he disapproved of the whole concept of Resolutions at any time of year. He chose to see this current exercise more in the light of a 'Note to Self' rather than drawing up commandments to restrict his future behaviour. Settling to his task, he began to write with a flourish, being fond of lavishness.

Point One:

While it is necessary in these current times to be wary of excessive spending, I may have been a tad too parsimonious this festive season. In future, I shall seek out a better-quality dinner. No more old birds for me! The meat was stringy, the bones thin and marrowless, the giblets wizened. No amount of the black sausage, plump dumplings and thick Red Eye Gravy I added later could compensate for those shortcomings. I must accept that I will need to focus on snaring younger birds in the future in order to sate my tastes.

Point Two:

I must adopt a regular self-care programme. Skilful hairstyling would help to disguise those horrible large ears I've inherited from Grandpa Lupin, and I really must do something about my teeth. I haven't been to the Dentist in years. Capping them maybe … but certainly a descaling to remove that unpleasant yellowish tinge. As for waxing, well… my forearms and legs are long overdue.

Point Three:

I've been pondering it for years but I really must think of moving. Those Woodcutters are completely overrunning this neck of the forest. There's far too many of them now. Coming here in search of work indeed! Have they no trees where they come from? I can hardly stroll down a single pathway without having to hide from lumber carts. And the noise! Shouting, trees crashing, sawing … it's all too much. I'll have to find somewhere else altogether, where I can go quietly about my business without interference.

Point Four:

Sugared food is not for me. When will I learn? I scoffed all the sweet treats in the basket after dinner last night, and how I've paid for it all day! Such indigestion! I know Mama always said Diabetes runs in our family. I really need to get medical advice on my diet.

Four Points were quite enough. Bored as he so often became, he threw down the quill, heading for the cottage door. Gazing out he smirked a sinister smile, wondering if his Wolf brothers were ready yet to play with him on that beautiful moonlit night.

her new whiskey bottle

~ after 'Labelled with Love',
sung by Squeeze, 1981 ~

The Stimulus: Write song lyrics based on the first line of an actual song

she unscrews the top from her new whiskey bottle
sniffs brown velvet Lethe   tantilizing respite
a slow steady onset into kindly oblivion
a cracked clouded glass is filled to its rim
shunning the pretention of inch high shots
liquored bloodstream the aim why bother to posture
who cares it's the taste of the cheapest bought
she seeks anaesthetic   solace sought

since he's been gone she feels owed some reprieve
from the pain of his absence   being a reject ex-wife
blunted sounds filter in from an outside street
underlining the pain of a lonely heartbeat
the power of the malt pads the walls of her world
blurs the prison hours passed on the edge of a knife
she freefalls into sleep   dark insensate empty
but each morning wakes up to again unscrew
the top of her new whiskey bottle.

a canine acrostic

~ a dog walk when it is snowing ~

(Human - English, Canine - translation provided)

And you wanted to come out in this!

Don't blame me. If I've to pee, I've to pee.

Oh that ole line. Why can't you just cross your paws!?!

God, when will you learn. I've only a tiny bladder. I've held on as long as I can.

Well, it's not long enough. I was very comfortable in that armchair doing the Crossword.

All right, I'll go on the carpet the next time.

Like you did last week?

Kitchen door was shut or I'd have gone on the tiles. We both know that's easier to clean.

Well, you didn't. I was on my knees for hours with the steamer and hairdryer.

Her daft idea, buying that fancy thick white carpet.

Ever consider she only choose a Pomeranian so the hairs

wouldn't show?

Nope. One look at me and she was in love. Just like you.

I fell in love? That's drastically overplaying it, don't you think. You're still on probation.

That Back-to-the-Dealer threat wore thin weeks ago. You know you love me.

In this weather! Don't push your luck.

So what, you're a bit wet and cold? Just look at how gorgeous I am in my fur coat.

Soaked to the skin, me. Probably get my death.

Now stop being such a drama queen. We'll be back at the House in a few minutes.

Out in this weather for an ungrateful mut like you. I must be mad!

Would you rather be stuck with just her Sphinx cat as a pet!?!

It certainly seems a better option at the moment.

Now look, we're back at the Front Door. You can stop whinging.

Get inside. That's your last walk today. No, don't look at me like that. This time I mean it.

The Hawthorn Tree

the hawthorn tree drooped to
nuzzle the ground   strained to caress
the grass in its perfect circle   the lure of safe magic
beckoned below the canopy   the branches whispered
a multi stringed symphony of overlapping voices
those who had planted those who had protected
those who had come for sanctuary
behind the music a gentle harmony
of presences layered enchantment
we are here   they chorused
with a gentle flutter
of gossamer wings
and a
light
breeze
of
fairie

A Camino at St Anne's Cathedral

Winding through the lives
the deaths
the remembered
wearing the shell of a pilgrim
the Visitor walks on geometric marbling
soft summer shoes create no sound
into that void the echoes fall
images of colour
light
brightness
hue flicker
but peripheral vision glimpses a shadow
a pass-by from windows of
Patience
Charity
Peace

the echoes come
not just from past memories
but from the ceremonies of now-
a baby's cry from a christening
a tight sob escaping at a funeral
the shuffling of childish feet
eager to escape the sermon

as the Visitor walks
layers are stripped
discarded on the floor in tattered shrouds
of the outside
the mundane
the white noise
of everyday life

as they drop
a raw core rises to the surface
to be stroked by calm essence
hushed grace
a sense of the important truths

in an ambulatory journey
the Visitor is rebirthing
going back into the one soul
the connectivity of humanity
the knowledge of how to be
not what we appear
but what we are

Breathe and push! let the amoeba pulse and grow

Printed in Great Britain
by Amazon

37527221R00175